ask emma

FRENEMIES

SHERYL BERK
& CARRIE BERK

YELLOW
JACKET

This is a work of fiction. Any references to historical events, real
people, or real places are used fictitiously. Other names, characters,
places, and events are products of the author's imagination, and any
resemblance to actual events or places or persons, living or dead, is
entirely coincidental.

YELLOW JACKET
an imprint of Bonnier Publishing USA

251 Park Avenue South, New York, NY 10010
Copyright © 2019 by Sheryl Berk & Carrie Berk
All rights reserved, including the right of reproduction
in whole or in part in any form.
Yellow Jacket is a trademark of Bonnier Publishing USA, and associated
colophon is a trademark of Bonnier Publishing USA.
Manufactured in the United States of America BVG 0119
First Edition

1 3 5 7 9 10 8 6 4 2

Library of Congress Cataloging-in-Publication Data
is available upon request.
ISBN 978-1-4998-0648-9
yellowjacketreads.com
bonnierpublishingusa.com

To Aunt Peggy,

For who you are and all you do . . . we love you

1

THE GOOD OLE DAYS AT ARMADILLO

Emma Woods kept a calendar above her desk, turning the pages of months and X-ing off the days until one small box in June finally read, "0 Days to Camp Armadillo!" The animal-themed day camp in the nearby Sweetland Mountains had been her summer home since she was five years old, a place filled with fun and friends and ice pops on sweltering-hot afternoons. It was where she learned to swim and dive; it was where she mastered making friendship bracelets and lanyard key chains. It was where she played her first starring role onstage: Belle in *Beauty and the Beast*. All of her best memories of being a kid were from Camp Armadillo—she proudly wore her camp T-shirt year-round and loved to sing the official camp cheer:

> *Chick-Chick-Chickadee,*
> *Hippo, Moose, and Monkey!*
> *Everyone come say our chant—you know it's*
>   *pretty funky!*
> *We wear our camp shirts oh-so-proud whether*
>   *Elephant or Cheetah,*
> *We swim and boat and play all day,*
> *We're always on our feet-a!*
> *Give a cheer! Give a cry! Give a whoop-de-do!*
> *Armadillo, Armadillo, we love you!*

Armadillo was Emma's, hers to love and treasure and look forward to all year long. When she became a sixth grader at Austen Middle School, her parents reminded her she was too big to be a camper anymore—eleven was the absolute age limit. Luckily, there were other options!

She closed her eyes and recalled how last summer, she and her best friend, Harriet Horowitz, signed up to be Armadillo counselors in training (CITs). Harriet had all sorts of allergies—pollen, ragweed, mold—and was a little nervous about being "in the outdoors all day." But Emma convinced her it would be a blast.

"It's just like babysitting—with benefits," she assured her. Yes, they had to supervise the tiny Chickadee groups in the water and make sure they didn't cry, fight, or swallow half the pool. But they also had CIT free swim, all-you-can-eat lunch, their very own bunk with lockers, and the annual staff trip to Hersheypark.

Emma loved the idea of being a CIT; it made her feel like a grown-up. Sure, there was a tremendous amount of responsibility, but there was also a lot of freedom, a summer paycheck ($250!), and tips from parents who were eager to have her keep "a special eye" on their kids.

"So Mrs. Marbutz gave me five dollars this morning to make sure little Mikey doesn't get teased by his fellow Monkeys," Emma told Harriet as she climbed into the camp bus and took a seat next to her. "The kids call him Mar-butthead," Emma whispered. "What am I supposed to do about that?"

Harriet seemed preoccupied with applying her bug spray and sunscreen. "I burn very easily," she complained, showing Emma a red splotch on her shoulder. "Look at this! This was just from walking the Cheetahs yesterday to lunch. I was in the sun for five minutes, and look at me!"

In Emma's opinion, Harriet had it easy: She was a CIT for arts and crafts. Most of the day, she was inside the air-conditioned studio, handing out colored paper, pipe cleaners, glue, and markers. Emma, on the other hand, was in charge of the five-year-old-girl group. Not only did she have to chaperone them to nature, archery, horseback riding, and assorted sports, but she also took them to and from the bathroom, making sure they washed their hands and didn't fall into the toilet!

"You know what I love most about being a CIT?" Emma asked her.

"Let me guess," Harriet scoffed. "The bugs, the sunburn, the whiny campers with runny noses . . ."

"No," Emma said, putting her arm around her bestie. "Getting to hang with my BFF all summer long."

"Okay," Harriet said. "That's reasonable. But I miss Izzy."

The third member of their BFF trio, Isabelle Park, was at gymnastics sleepaway camp for eight weeks. And she barely had time to write either of them a letter—except to mention that she met a cute boy named Ben, who was captain of his middle school gymnastics team.

"I know. I miss her too," Emma said. At school, the

three of them were virtually inseparable, and it had been that way since they first met in kindergarten.

"What do you think Izzy is doing right now?" Emma wondered aloud.

"Not sitting in a bus filled with five-year-olds," Harriet said, "praying one of them doesn't get bus-sick." Emma glanced over at Mikey Marbutz. He did look a little green, and that would make the third time this week.

Harriet dug a bottle of sanitizer out of her bag and poured it on her hands. "Why do little kids have to be so gross?"

"We were that little once," Emma said. "Remember?"

"Little, yes. Gross, no!"

"Remember the time in first grade when you dumped chocolate milk all over yourself and Izzy, right before we took class pictures? That was pretty gross!"

"It was an accident," Harriet replied. "My hands were slippery. Those crackers they gave us at snack time were very greasy."

Emma couldn't help but giggle at the memory of Harriet in her white lace dress and Izzy in her pink satin one, both with big brown stains on their skirts. "You guys smelled like sour milk all day!"

Harriet dotted some calamine lotion on another bite on her ankle. "I'd take school and sour milk over this any day."

"Earth to Emma!"

Fingers snapped in her face and Emma's eyes flew open. She was at a crowded table in the cafeteria—not at Armadillo, her happy place. She noticed Harriet was sipping a carton of chocolate milk.

"Did you hear a single word I said?" Izzy asked impatiently. "What planet were you on?"

It took a moment for Emma to recall they were now back in school, halfway through the seventh grade, and the next summer at Armadillo was several months away.

"I was just daydreaming about last summer," she said with a sigh. "It was so much fun."

"Speak for yourself," Harriet complained. "It was itchy and hot and filled with germs."

"Harriet begs to differ," Izzy said, chuckling. "You sure you guys went to the same place?"

"But you'll be an Armadillo CIT with me next summer, right?" Emma practically begged Harriet.

"Nope," Harriet insisted. "I can't do it again. I'm still having nightmares."

"Oh no!" Honestly, sometimes Harriet could be so closed-minded. "But you were a great CIT!" Emma assured her friend. "You have to do it again."

Emma turned to Izzy for support.

"You can't convince me either," Izzy warned her. "So don't even try."

"I wasn't going to," Emma fibbed. But she was— she was going to try to convince both of them, even if it took the rest of seventh grade to do so. How much fun would it be to have both her BFFs at Armadillo next summer—and it was only 153 days away!

"I'm not even sure what an armadillo looks like," Izzy admitted.

"It's got this hard shell with rings on it and a long, pointy tail and snout," Harriet explained. "It's not very attractive at all."

"It doesn't matter what it looks like," Emma defended her camp. "It's an awesome place to spend the summer with friends!"

Harriet shook her head emphatically. "Not gonna happen again . . . ever. Honestly, Ems, sometimes you can be a little too pushy."

"Hah! A little?" Izzy said. "Try a *lot*!"

Emma scowled. "That's not true."

"Really?" Izzy challenged her. "How about your *Ask Emma* advice blog? Isn't that telling everyone what to do?"

From the moment Emma had launched *Ask Emma* on Austen Middle's website a few months ago, people questioned her motives—even her BFFs and her own brother. But blogging wasn't about her. She wanted to help people with their problems, and she was really good at giving advice and sorting things out.

"Iz, you know everyone likes *Ask Emma*," Harriet said, piping up in Emma's defense. Then she paused. *"Now."*

As much as Emma hated to admit, her friend was right—both of them were. In the beginning, there had been snide remarks and nasty comments from her peers. Then things escalated into cyberbullying, and her parents were even called into the principal's office. Emma could have given up right then, but instead she decided to use her experience to make a difference.

"I know, I know—it was a pretty bad situation at first," she admitted. "But in the end, I did get everyone to sign the Say No to Cyberbullying Student Contract." She had also gained the respect of her classmates and one boy in particular—Jackson Knight. The new kid in school had started off as perplexing as an advanced algebra problem, yet wound up as one of Emma's biggest supporters.

Izzy relented. "Fine, I'm just saying that sometimes you get too involved in other people's lives instead of focusing on your own problems."

"Problems? What problems?"

Izzy motioned toward a table in the back of the cafeteria where Jackson was sitting with some of the other boys from their grade.

Emma blushed. She had thought about asking Jackson to sit with her at lunch today but wondered if that would be too bold a move.

"Leave Emma alone," Harriet tried to hush Izzy. "Her love life is none of our business."

"But she sticks *her* nose into my love life all the time!" Izzy insisted. "And remember how she tried to fix you up with Elton?"

Harriet shuddered at the thought. "Marty is so much more my type than Elton. He's into comics and *Star Wars,* and we're allergic to practically all the same things!"

Emma shrugged. She meant well and was happy that Harriet had a boyfriend—even if Marty hadn't been her first choice for her BFF. Meddling was simply something Emma couldn't control. She wanted everyone, especially her two closest friends, to find love—the wonderful, sweep-you-off-your-feet romance that Elizabeth and Mr. Darcy shared in *Pride and Prejudice*. It was the best movie she'd ever seen. Her mom had suggested they watch the miniseries ("Colin Firth is simply dreamy") one week when they were both home sick with the flu. Emma had protested at first—but then she fell in love with the story after the very first episode.

Despite her appreciation for old-fashioned romance, she had been too busy matchmaking for others to even think about a boyfriend for herself—until Jackson walked into her life and took the locker next to hers. Little by little, she had gained his trust. His affection, however, was a whole other story. That might take a little more finessing. For now, they were friends. Good friends.

"What would *Ask Emma* advise you?" Harriet

asked her. "Would she tell you to go up to Jax and say hi or play hard to get?"

Emma considered. "I think she would say, 'Don't play games. Honesty is the best and only policy when it comes to relationships.'"

Izzy snickered. "Until he thinks you're a stalker. Or meets someone else and forgets you even exist."

"Nice job, Iz."—Harriet elbowed her—"Way to ruin the romance."

"I'm just being practical," she insisted.

"She's just being negative because the guy she met in sleepaway camp last summer didn't work out," Harriet pointed out.

"I couldn't care less about Ben," Izzy said, sounding more than a little defensive. "I hope he has a great life without me."

Emma kept staring in Jackson's direction until she caught his eye . . . and he smiled.

"I'm going over there," she said, getting up from their table.

"Go get him!" Harriet cheered.

Izzy rolled her eyes. "Whatever."

Emma took a deep breath, crossed her fingers, and walked toward Jackson, who was now deep in discussion with Elton and two other boys.

Okay, she told herself, here goes nothing!

2

SECRETS AND LIES

"Hey!" Emma said cheerfully.

Jackson looked up from his conversation—why did he have to have such dreamy blue eyes?

"Hey," he answered. "What's up, Emma?"

She hovered over the table. "Um, not much. You?"

Jackson shrugged. "Nothin'."

Elton jumped in. "You're way too modest, dude! Jax got picked to represent Austen Middle at the National Student Congress."

Emma raised an eyebrow. "Student Congress? What's that?"

Jackson blushed. "It's nothing."

"Are you kidding me?" Elton exclaimed. "It's like the smartest kids in the country coming together to debate important stuff."

"What sort of important stuff?" Emma pressed.

Jackson looked very uncomfortable with the conversation. She could tell because he kept running his hands through his dark wavy hair.

"You know—issues," Elton explained. "The things that kids have to deal with."

Issues? Things kids have to deal with? Wasn't this what *Ask Emma* was about? And why was Jackson going and not *her*?

"I don't understand." Emma tried to stay calm. "How did *you* get picked?"

Jackson shrugged. "I dunno. I mean, Mr. Carter,

my history teacher, submitted my name to Ms. Bates and he just told me today I'm going."

"To Washington, DC!" Elton interjected. "For a whole weekend! And they get to see the Lincoln Memorial at night and go to a huge after-party!"

Emma could feel the anger bubbling up inside her. She stared at Jackson. Had he not planned on telling her any of this? She *thought* they were past all of this. When Jackson first came to Austen, he barely revealed anything about himself. But slowly, Emma had gotten him to trust her. This felt like a lie—and a huge step backward.

"It's really no biggie," Jackson assured her. "I'm just kind of into American history and government stuff, and Mr. Carter thought I would make a good representative."

"Right," Emma snapped back, completely forgetting that she had come over to his table to flirt. "You'll make a great representative with no experience dealing with student issues or figuring things out. You're super qualified!"

"Woah!" Elton said, whistling through his teeth. "That's harsh!"

"Emma, it's not like I purposely tried to one-up you on this," Jackson said.

"Didn't you? You could have turned it down, Jax. You could have suggested that they send *me*. That would have been the nice thing to do!"

Jackson considered. "Well, yeah. But I want to go. I've never been to DC and Student Congress sounds pretty awesome."

Emma froze in her tracks. So a trip to DC was more important than *her*? "You go right ahead," she shouted. "You go to DC. Have a great time!"

"Gee, someone's not a happy camper . . . ," Elton said, snickering. "Take it easy, Emma."

"You butt out of this!" she shouted at Elton. "All you want to do is rub my nose in the fact that I'm not going. I thought we were friends!"

"Emma, wait!" She heard Jackson calling after her as she marched away in a huff. She made a beeline out of the cafeteria so no one would see the steam coming out of her ears. She was furious! If anyone was going to represent Austen Middle at a Student Congress and talk about kids' issues, it should be her—she handed out advice every day! She was the one who was sympathetic and compassionate and focused on fixing things that were broken. This was simply not acceptable! Emma barged into Principal Bates's office, prepared to argue her case.

"Ms. Bates, we need to talk," she said, storming in.

"Emma," Ms. Bates said between mouthfuls of her ham-and-cheese sandwich. "Come in. Oh, wait— you *are* in. Without knocking." By now, Ms. Bates was used to Emma's impassioned outbursts—usually to right a wrong or inform her principal of a situation that needed immediate attention.

"I'm sorry, but this simply can't wait," Emma said, taking a seat across from the principal.

Ms. Bates sighed. "It never can. What is it now?"

"Why am I not going?"

"Going where?"

"To the National Student Congress. Why is

Jackson Knight going and not me?"

Ms. Bates took a sip of tea. "Emma, I know you are very passionate about helping your peers—"

"Passionate? It's what I live for!" Emma replied. "When someone feels bad, I feel bad for them, and I can't stand by and not do something! I am an expert problem-fixer, Ms. Bates!"

"I get that. But the National Student Congress requires a cool head and a calm demeanor," her principal explained. "It requires someone who can discuss important topics facing today's youth without getting, well, worked up about them."

"Oh." Emma suddenly realized her rant wasn't really helping. "Well, I can do that," she assured her principal.

Ms. Bates sat back in her chair. "Really?"

"Absolutely!" Emma insisted. "I can be completely calm and cool and unemotional."

"You left out open-minded and unbiased," Ms. Bates added. "When you sit on Student Congress, they want you to listen objectively and consider all sides of the issues. They want an open discussion—not a screaming match. Some problems aren't a quick fix; they're not black and white."

"I love gray," Emma said, pointing to her sweatshirt's smoky hue. "See?"

"You have some very strong opinions, Emma," Ms. Bates continued. "I admire that as well as your ability to express those opinions. But I'm not sure you'd let any of the other members of Student Congress get a word in!"

"I can zip my lip," Emma said, miming a zipper across her mouth. "And I can prove it."

Ms. Bates tapped her fingers on her mug. "How can you prove it?"

Emma thought for a moment. "I will completely keep my opinions to myself for forty-eight hours. Even if I feel very strongly about something, I will stay neutral."

"Fine," Ms. Bates said, taking another bite of her sandwich. "You stay impartial for forty-eight hours and I'll consider sending you to Student Congress as well. I have to choose a second student and I already have a few strong candidates."

"I'm the strongest!" Emma insisted. "Really. I can prove it to you."

"Fine," Ms. Bates said. "I'll be keeping a close eye on you—and your blog."

Her blog! Emma had completely forgotten she had promised her readers that she would write another post by the end of the week. And it was already Wednesday.

"About that," she began. "Maybe the staying-impartial part could just refer to spoken, not written, advice?"

Ms. Bates shook her head. "Both—or it's a no-go on Washington."

"Fine," Emma agreed. "I can totally be Sweden."

Ms. Bates chuckled. "Switzerland. I think you mean Switzerland. That's the neutral country that doesn't go to war."

"That too," Emma said, rising to her feet. "Just watch me."

3

MY LIPS ARE SEALED

If Ms. Bates wanted a cool-headed congresswoman, that was exactly what she was going to get. Sure, it would be tough to stifle her opinions, but forty-eight hours wasn't so long . . . was it?

"Hey, Em, how did it go with Jax?" Izzy asked, catching up to Emma at her friend's locker. "One minute you were talking to him, then—poof—you disappeared."

"I've got it under control," Emma replied.

"Good, because I have a problem—a huge problem. And I need your help." Izzy pulled her BFF aside next to the janitor's closet so they could talk without anyone overhearing. Emma gulped. It had only been a few minutes since her meeting with Ms. Bates and already the drama was starting.

"I'm late to class," Emma said, trying to avoid Izzy. "Can we talk later? Like maybe Friday night?" That was forty-eight hours away—she'd be in the clear by then.

"Friday? Are you kidding me? This is life-or-death!" Izzy insisted.

"Really? Life-or-death?" Emma asked, scanning the hallway to make sure Ms. Bates was nowhere in sight. "Okay, tell me."

"It's Harriet."

"What do you mean?" Emma asked. "I thought you said this was your problem."

"It is. Harriet is my problem."

Now Emma was totally confused! "How could Harriet be your problem?"

"Remember how we planned for you guys to come watch my gymnastics meet tomorrow after school, then go out for pizza after?"

Emma nodded. "Yeah, Harriet and I are really excited for it."

"Well, I thought about it, and I don't want Harriet there. I kind of told her that, and she started crying and now she's not speaking to me."

"What? Why would you tell her that?" Emma asked. She and Harriet always came to Izzy's big gymnastic meets.

"Because I don't want her to come," Izzy explained. "She gets all nervous and flustered and that makes me all nervous and flustered. She totally distracts me."

Izzy wasn't completely wrong. Emma recalled the last meet about a month before when she and Harriet had gone to cheer Izzy on. Every time Izzy mounted the balance beam, Harriet had pulled her hoodie over her head and hid her eyes. And when Izzy wobbled on her dismount, Harriet had screamed "Nooooooo!" from the bleachers and made a huge scene.

"Harriet means well . . . she just gets a little worried for you," Emma told Izzy.

"I know, but I can't worry about her worrying. I'm sorry, she can't come to any more of my meets. It stresses me out!"

Emma could see both sides: Harriet felt left out, and Izzy felt anxious. Ordinarily, she would have asked them both to come over after school and talk this out between them. They would bicker and eventually reach a solution—usually over several of her mom's chocolate chip cookies. But getting involved with her BFFs' drama was not staying Switzerland.

"I can't help. I'd like to, but I can't," she told Izzy.

"What? Why? Because you're on Harriet's side? Because you value her friendship more than you value mine? Because she's right and I'm wrong?

Because she went to Camp Armadillo with you last summer and I didn't?"

"No! None of the above!" Emma said, trying to explain. "I have to stay neutral and not say what I think."

"Aha! So you do agree with her—and you don't want to tell me," Izzy fumed. "Fine, Emma. Be that way. Consider yourself uninvited to my meet too."

Izzy stomped off and left Emma standing at the closet, wondering what had just happened.

Harriet came running up to her.

"Oh good! She left! She's being so mean!" Harriet blurted out. "You have to fix this, Em."

Emma shook her head. "I can't. I'd like to, but I really can't."

Harriet's eyes grew wide. "You think Izzy's right! You think I made her lose her last meet! You think I'm a terrible friend!"

"I didn't say that, Harriet," Emma tried to reassure her. "I didn't say anything."

"You don't have to!" Harriet said, sniffling. "You're taking her side."

"No! I'm not taking anyone's side!" Emma cried. Then she noticed Ms. Bates coming down the hallway and lowered her voice. "I just have to stay calm, cool, and impartial."

"Fine, if you and Izzy don't want to be my BFFs anymore, then that's fine. I don't need either of you." She ran to the bathroom in hysterics.

Emma wanted to run after Harriet, but Ms. Bates was watching her every move. As much as Emma felt bad for Harriet, she had told Ms. Bates she could easily keep her emotions in check and not get wrapped up in everyone's issues. Emma had to prove it.

"Everything okay, Emma?" Ms. Bates asked, seeing Harriet race past her.

"Fine, fine," Emma said. "Harriet and Izzy are having a little disagreement and I'm staying totally out of it—like I promised. I am not telling Izzy that she should be more considerate of her friend's feelings, and I am not telling Harriet that she has to put herself in Izzy's shoes. I am not telling either of them that they are being totally unreasonable and selfish and overreacting and I am not getting between them." Which is exactly where she was—stuck in the middle with neither of her BFFs speaking to her. It was a horrible situation and she hated that she had to wait forty-eight hours to fix it.

"Good," Ms. Bates said. "I'll go check on Harriet. Remember . . . Switzerland."

For the rest of the day, Emma felt like she was alone on a desert island: no Izzy, no Harriet, and no Jackson. And it felt really weird not to jump up and down in her seat in protest when Marty stated his ridiculous opinion in English class. But she had promised Ms. Bates.

"So, Winnie should have drunk the spring water and stayed young forever," Marty had said about *Tuck Everlasting*, the book they were reading. "I mean, come on! How cool would it be to never grow up?"

Emma rolled her eyes. She wanted to shout

"Everyone should grow up and stop acting like big babies!" Instead, she stifled a yawn.

Mrs. Cole stared in her direction. "Anyone have something to say about that?" she asked pointedly. Emma knew what her teacher was expecting. This was the part of class when Emma would usually wave her hand wildly in the air to challenge Marty's opinion.

"Emma?" her teacher asked. "Are you feeling okay?"

Emma nodded. "Yup. I'm fine."

"You have nothing to say about Marty's theory?"

Emma took a deep breath. "Nope. Nothing."

Mrs. Cole scratched her head. "Really? That's not like you. You always have a very strong opinion about what we're discussing in English class."

"Not today," Emma insisted.

Marty beamed—Emma always shot his ideas down. This was a first!

The class then continued—very quietly and un-interrupted—until the bell rang.

Emma gathered up her books and backpack. Mrs. Cole was still puzzled over her student's behavior. "I hope you feel more like yourself tomorrow," she told Emma. "I'm not used to you being, well, quiet."

"Not tomorrow. But things will be back to normal Monday," she promised. If only she could fast-forward those forty-eight hours, everything would be fine again! She'd set Marty straight on *Tuck Everlasting*; she'd make Izzy and Harriet bury the hatchet, and she wouldn't be mad at Jackson anymore—they'd be planning their time in DC together!

When Emma left her English class, Ms. Bates was in the hall talking to a group of students but managed a friendly wave in Emma's direction.

Only two days, Emma told herself. Only two.

4

SWITZERLAND

Emma was relieved to be home, away from Ms. Bates's watchful glare. She opened the front door and found her brother and a bunch of his high school baseball-team buddies seated on the couch, playing video games.

"Oh no! The kid's home!" Luc announced as she walked by them.

"You're kids too," Emma reminded him. "You're only two years older than me."

"In dog years, that's fourteen," he teased her. "Feed Jagger, will ya? He looks hungry." Their family labradoodle ran anxiously in circles around Emma's feet.

"Come on, boy," she said to Jagger. "Let's see if Luc was eating your dog treats again."

"Not funny, Emma," Luc called after her. "You know I hate liver."

"Then I'll make sure to tell Mom to make it for dinner tonight," Emma tossed back at him. "Yummy liver and onions!"

"Uck!" Luc made a face. "Disgusting!" He threw a couch pillow at her and she ducked.

At least when she argued with her big brother, it was about silly stuff like liver. Luc had no interest in deeper discussions. When their dad had asked them over dinner what they thought about global warming, Luc had shrugged and said, "I didn't know the globe was cold. Maybe it could use a few blankets?" He was only half joking; he really didn't know what the issue was about.

"Luc, you're in high school," Mr. Woods said. "Isn't it about time you cared about something more than just sports? Maybe read a newspaper? Formulate some opinions?"

Emma couldn't have agreed more, but at the moment, she was incredibly jealous of her big brother: He was surrounded by a posse of pals, and she was with the dog. None of her friends wanted to be around her.

Luc read her mind. "So, where's Tweedle Dum and Tweedle Dumber?" he said, referring to Izzy and Harriet. "No playdate after school today?"

Emma bristled. Luc loved to make her out to be a baby—especially in front of his baseball buddies.

"They're busy. I'm busy," she said.

"Doing what? Painting your toenails?" Luc taunted her.

His friend Rich cackled. "Oh man. You're a riot, Luc!"

"For your information, I have a blog to write," she informed them.

"Hey, guys, who has a good question for *Ask Emma*?" Luc said. "Something really tough—so she'll go upstairs and work on answering it and get out of our faces."

Rich raised his hand like he was in class.

"Yes?" Emma said, slightly suspicious that they were playing her. But Rich *did* actually seem serious.

"So I want to take this job after school at Holbart's Sporting Goods, but my parents say I can't because I have to study. It's a really cool place to work and I'd make money to put toward the new iPhone I want."

"You left out the part where you're failing science," Luc reminded him.

"Oh yeah. But I'd be failing science whether I worked at Holbart's or not. My teacher hates my guts."

"Hmm," Emma contemplated. "That's a big problem."

"I know! So, what's your advice? I should take

the job, right? Tell my parents they're being unfair? Call my grandma and grandpa and get them on my side?" Rich asked.

Emma considered—then remembered her promise to stay neutral. "I can't say," she replied. "I mean, you have a point and so do your parents—all of you have good arguments."

"So, who's right?" Rich pressed her.

"I can't say," Emma repeated.

Luc leaned forward. "You can't say? Since when? You always have something to say—too much if you ask me. You never stop talking, even when no one asks you for your opinion."

"Well, I'm not saying—at least not today or tomorrow," she insisted, leading Jagger into the kitchen.

"Weird," Luc said, taking a handful of popcorn. "You're acting really weird!"

Emma felt weird. Normally, she would have told Rich to work out a deal with his parents: He would study hard when he wasn't working and raise his grade in science to prove to them he could handle both school and a job. She would have told him to sit his parents down and let them know how important this was to him—and how it was good for him to gain experience and a sense of responsibility. She could have come up with a million reasons why his parents should reconsider—arguing a case was her specialty. But arguing wouldn't get her in Ms. Bates's good graces—or on a train to DC.

"Liver or chicken flavor?" she asked Jagger, fishing into his treat jar. The dog barked his response. "I see! You want both! That's being very impartial." She patted him on the head. "Good boy."

Just then her mom came in carrying a large bag of groceries. "Emma, honey, can you help me unpack these and get dinner going? Your dad will be home any minute and he'll be starved. He had two surgeries this afternoon."

Emma's father was a cardiologist—a fixer of broken hearts. Maybe he could do something about the gnawing feeling she had in her heart every time she thought of Jackson. Surely, he hated her for telling him off today at lunch. Why had she lost her temper with him? He hadn't asked to be chosen for Student Congress; he hadn't purposely taken her spot. Yet in the heat of the moment, when Elton was rubbing it in her face, she couldn't stop the anger from flooding over her and the words from pouring out of her mouth. Now, looking back on it, maybe she could have handled things differently and supported Jackson. It wasn't his fault, and she had acted like it was. Maybe Ms. Bates was right—if she couldn't control her emotions, she didn't belong on the National Student Congress. Maybe she shouldn't even be writing an advice blog!

"Honey, you seem a little distracted," her mother said, noticing that Emma had just placed a bag of Doritos in the freezer.

"I am. I had a bad day," she answered.

"Well, we all have bad days. You have to let it go," she said, planting a kiss on Emma's forehead. "Things will look better tomorrow."

"I doubt it," Emma said. Tomorrow promised to be more of the same. Jackson would still hate her, Harriet and Izzy would still be icing her out, and she would still have to wait for Monday before she could even attempt to fix any of it.

"Do you want to talk about it?" her mom asked. "I can be impartial."

Emma groaned. "Don't use that word! I hate *impartial*. I hate not being able to get excited about something that makes me excited. Calm is seriously overrated!"

Mrs. Woods put down the quart of milk she was holding. "Impartial doesn't mean you have to keep your mouth shut," she explained. "It means you have to consider all sides and be fair, think before you speak."

"So you're saying I'm not fair?"

"I'm saying that when you make your mind up, it's hard to convince you otherwise," her mom said. "But that's not a bad thing. You're a girl who stands her ground."

"I am," Emma said. "And I shouldn't have to miss out on DC because of it."

"DC? Do you want to tell me what this is about?" her mom asked.

"It's about me. Ms. Bates doesn't believe I have what it takes to be on the National Student Congress in DC. She said I would get too fired up and I wouldn't let anyone get a word in."

"Aha." Her mom nodded. "So that's why you need to practice being impartial."

"Yes! I'm supposed to prove I can be Switzerland for forty-eight hours—and it's ruining my life! Everyone hates me because I can't say anything! You can ask Emma, but I can't answer!"

"Well, it's only temporary," her mom said. She handed her a package of cheese from the grocery bag. "You might as well have some Swiss if you're going to be Switzerland."

For the first time that entire day, Emma smiled. Her mom was really good at putting things into perspective—and brightening an otherwise dismal day with a really bad joke.

"Switzerland goes really great with ham and mustard," Mrs. Woods teased.

"I think I would prefer it on a tuna melt," Emma bantered back.

Her mom grilled her a sandwich, and they split the snack.

"You can find a happy medium—a way to state your opinions in a fair, nonjudgmental way without getting swept up in a tizzy," her mom said. "Sometimes people hear you better if you whisper instead of shout."

"It's so hard!" Emma said. "Sometimes I just open my mouth and things come flying out."

"I know. It's because you care so much about so much," her mom said. "You've got a big heart, Emma. You just have to learn how and when to unleash your amazing Emma-ness on the world." She ruffled her hair. "Get it?"

Emma chewed on a piece of crust. "Got it.

And I think I'm going to try writing a post on my blog tonight."

"Good for you." Her mom patted her on the back. "I'm sure it will be a great one."

Emma wasn't so sure—but she knew she had to give it a try.

Emma scanned her inbox for a question from one of her peers that didn't work her up in "a tizzy." There was one from a boy who thought recess should be an hour longer every day ("my brain needs the rest"); another was from a girl who insisted the girls' bathroom sink on the third floor was always clogged ("I got splashed yesterday!"). While neither of these topics got her particularly fired up (a good thing), neither inspired a post (a bad thing). Then she saw what she was looking for:

Emma, I need your help! I heard my supposed

BFF talking about me to other kids behind my back. She said some really mean things and I don't know whether I should say something or pretend everything is still okay between us.

Wow, Emma thought. This is a serious situation! That friend is no friend! She's a frenemy! She felt her heart race a little and her fingertips start to twitch—a sure sign that this would be a great new post the minute she began typing it. Then she remembered her promise not to get *too* worked up . . .

Instead, she typed:

Dear Potty Problems,

Clogged drains can be very frustrating! I mean, you go to wash your hands and the whole sink floods over and the cute outfit you picked to wear that morning suddenly has a big wet stain on the front. I hear ya. I'd recommend going to talk to Mr. Hansen, the head custodian, and letting him know there's an issue. I'm sure he can unclog it in no time. If the issue continues, clearly it's a plumbing problem that might need a professional's attention, in which case Mr. Hansen will have to make the call. It happens. One time, my brother flushed a water balloon down our toilet at home, and our whole second floor was practically underwater. My dad tried plunging and nada; the clog wouldn't come loose and the water kept flowing. We had to get a professional plumber in to snake the pipes, and he found this big, blue popped balloon stuffing everything up. It was a huge mess, but we got through it and Luc got grounded for a week.

Emma sighed. Her post seemed ridiculous. Why would anyone care that Luc flushed a balloon? Why would anyone be worried about a flood at Austen Middle? The sinks and toilets were always clogging, and Mr. Hansen was a whiz at fixing them. She reread what she wrote: It felt calm, cool, and impartial. She set it to post. It would simply have to do.

5

THREE'S A CROWD

The next morning, Emma was surprised to see Izzy
and Harriet huddled by the water fountain together.
This was the best news ever! They had fixed things
between them and all was well again!

"Yay, you're talking!" she said to them.

Izzy frowned. "We're talking to each other. Not
to you."

"Wait . . . what?" Emma replied, confused.

Harriet nodded. "We made up and we agree you don't care about either of us."

"Of course I care," Emma insisted. "I know you're mad at me, but I can explain: I promised Ms. Bates I would stay neutral for forty-eight hours so I could be a representative at the National Student Congress in DC. I have a whole day left and I have to mind my own business."

"Well, it won't be a problem then," Izzy replied, "because we don't need you involved in our lives. Period."

Emma couldn't believe what she was hearing! They were totally blowing things out of proportion! This wasn't her fault—couldn't they see that? Then she remembered how she had overreacted with Jackson, blaming him for something that wasn't his fault either. It was so easy to get swept up in emotions and say things you didn't mean.

"Guys, come on! This is me, Emma! Your bestie?"

"You mean former bestie," Harriet said. "You deserted both of us when we needed you."

How could Emma make them understand that none of this had been intentional—when Izzy and Harriet seemed stubbornly determined to punish her?

"But look!" Emma said. "You worked things out by yourselves! I'm so proud of you."

"Which proves we don't need to ask Emma anything anymore," Izzy said. "I called Harriet last night and said I was sorry and re-invited her to my meet."

"And I told Izzy I was sorry and would sit way in the back so I don't make her nervous."

"I'll come too!" Emma volunteered. "I'll even buy the pizza after the meet."

"No thanks," Harriet replied. "We're having a sleepover at my house."

"Oh! That will be so much fun!" Emma said enthusiastically. "Let's watch movie musicals!"

Izzy moved in closer to Emma until they were standing nose to nose. "You're missing the point. You're not invited."

"You really hurt our feelings, Emma," Harriet

added. "I always thought I could count on you, and you made me feel"—she paused—"like I didn't matter."

Before Emma could say another word in her defense, her friends turned their backs and walked away, arm in arm.

This was ridiculous! A huge misunderstanding! Emma was happy that her friends were together again, but she hadn't meant for their trio to become a duo. Emma walked to her locker and saw that Jackson was there, closing his beneath it. She braced herself for another ugly fight. But instead, Jackson just stood there, staring at her.

"Say something," she pleaded with him. "Izzy and Harriet aren't talking to me. I can't take the silence."

"Was it worth it?" he asked her calmly.

"Worth what?"

"Ruining all your friendships so you could go to some stupid Student Congress?" Clearly, he had seen the confrontation with Harriet and Izzy.

"Student Congress isn't stupid. You want to go."

"Not enough to hurt someone important to me," he said. "I told Ms. Bates this morning I want to give up my seat so you could go in my place."

"You did what?!" Emma cried. "I never told you to do that."

Jackson rested a hand on her shoulder. "You didn't have to."

Emma didn't know what to say—she had never intended to take Jackson's place. This felt wrong, horribly wrong. "Please! You have to go tell her you changed your mind and want your spot back!"

"Well, I am going . . ."

"She said no?" Emma asked. "So you still get to go to DC?"

"Don't sound so disappointed."

"I'm not. I mean, I am disappointed that I don't have a spot. But I'm happy you're still going. You shouldn't have to make that big of a sacrifice for me."

Jackson combed his hair out of his eyes. "Well, maybe I wanted to. Maybe you're worth it, Emma." He smiled before heading off to class, and she smiled back. Things between them were back on track, and all she wanted to do was run and tell Izzy and Harriet.

Emma could barely concentrate in math. Every word problem reminded her of her own problems:

If Mary has 128 gumballs and wants to keep ¼ and share the rest with her 2 best friends, how much will each friend get?

If Izzy had any gumballs, one thing would be certain: Now she would only share them with Harriet, not her! Emma had to figure this out. Not just the equation, but how to get herself back into her friends' good graces. The answer seemed easy on both fronts: Mary would have 32 gumballs, her 2 friends would each have 48, and Emma needed to write a new post—fast!

Instead of going to lunch and eating alone, Emma grabbed a yogurt and hid in the computer lab. She started typing:

It all began over a Barbie—the very first fight I had in kindergarten with my two BFFs (let's call them Lizzy and Hattie), and it was a doozy. It was Hattie's fifth birthday party, and her parents got her the Barbie doll of her dreams—Birthday Wishes Barbie, dressed in a flowing pink off-the-shoulder ball gown that lit up if you pressed a button on her back. I was totally in awe, but Lizzy had a different opinion.

"I don't like your doll," she told Hattie. "If someone gave me that for a present, I'd give it back—or throw it away."

"Lizzy, you don't mean that," I interjected.

"Yes, I do!" Lizzy insisted. "Why is her hair brown and not blonde? And her skirt is too poofy. Yuck!"

Hattie's lower lip trembled and I knew she was about to burst into tears.

"Say you're sorry," I whispered to Lizzy, trying to prevent the birthday girl from having a meltdown before she even blew out the candles on her cake.

"Sorry? I'm not saying sorry. It's true. That doll is ugly and I hate it."

There was no persuading Lizzy to apologize, so I knew it was up to me: "Hattie," I said, "that's the prettiest Barbie in the whole world and you are so lucky."

Hattie sniffled. "Really? You think so?"

"Absolutely!" I told her. "For my birthday, I'm asking for the very same one. So our dolls can be twins!"

Lizzy pouted and marched off into a corner. I knew that if there was one thing my friend couldn't stand, it was feeling like an outsider. Even at five years old, Lizzy had serious FOMO. But there was no other way to soothe Hattie's hurt feelings. I had to side with her—it was, after all, her special day.

Then Hattie went and did something totally unexpected: She walked over to where Lizzy was sulking and gently handed her the doll. "Don't be sad, Lizzy. We can share my present if you want." Hattie had completely forgotten that her friend had just dissed her doll in front of everyone. For the record, Hattie has the biggest heart—and even if it means that heart gets broken from time to time, it doesn't stop her from putting it out there.

Lizzy took the doll and all was forgiven. They skipped off hand in hand and ignored everyone else the rest of the party—including me. That's when I realized something: in refereeing between my two friends, I'd actually erased myself from the equation. Suddenly I was invisible. So I got mad. Really, really mad. I marched over and yanked the Barbie right out of Lizzy's hands, and in doing so, ripped the doll's arm right off. Hattie was hysterically crying, but luckily, her mom had some Krazy Glue and did emergency surgery. Barbie was as good as new.

Still, things were tense between all of us for at least a week. Hattie was totally traumatized, and Lizzy hated how I had sided against her—so it was payback time. My two BFFs had playdates after school every day without me. If it hadn't been for Hattie's mom finally inviting me to a sleepover with the two of them, it could have easily turned into World War Barbie. When we were finally back together as a trio, things felt right in the world again. We forgot our fight; we forgot what the fuss had been about. We stayed up all night gabbing and watching Hannah Montana episodes. A year later, none of us even wanted to play with dolls anymore. Barbie was bygones, and so was our fight and any hard feelings.

What is the point of this post besides reminiscing about my elementary school days and a plastic doll now buried somewhere in Hattie's basement? The point is, friends fight. Over Barbies, over boys, over misunderstandings. They sometimes say things they don't mean, and people get hurt in the process. Why? Because we love and care about one another deeply. If we didn't, it wouldn't hurt so much. But you can't let it pull you apart. You can't get hung up on who said what or who did what; none of that matters. What matters is the bond that's between you—it's stronger than Krazy Glue. Think about it.

XO,
Emma

6
WORDS GET IN THE WAY

Emma couldn't wait for Friday to finally arrive; it meant the end of her agreement with Ms. Bates, and, hopefully, her reconciliation with Izzy and Harriet. By now she was pretty certain they had read her blog—a blast went out every Friday morning announcing a new post. Even though she had changed their names, she was sure they would figure out what she was trying to tell them and would be touched.

Emma walked into Austen Middle a little earlier

than usual that Friday morning hoping that her BFFs would be waiting at her locker to hug her. But she had no such luck.

"Looking for me?" Elton asked, appearing out of nowhere.

"No, actually I was looking for Izzy or Harriet. Or both."

"Haven't seen them. But I did read your post. I forgive you."

Emma raised an eyebrow. "*You* forgive *me*?"

"Yes, I can see how much you blame yourself for what happened between us."

Emma was utterly confused. "What are you talking about, Elton?"

He put a hand on her shoulder. "Have you forgotten the little scene you made in the cafeteria? How you yelled at me and stormed out?"

Emma shook her head in disbelief. Did Elton honestly think the post was all about him? Was he that clueless?

"Elton, I—"

"Want to apologize. That's very big of you, Emma, and like I said, I forgive you."

Emma shook her head. "I should apologize? You got me upset over Student Congress and that's why I got into a fight with Jax, Izzy, Harriet—"

Elton held his hand up to hush her protests. "We've been friends since kindergarten, and I'm not gonna let this come between us. I can read between the lines of your post and I accept your apology for telling me off."

Emma rolled her eyes. He'd read her post all wrong! But the last thing she needed was another person hating her guts.

"Oh yes, you're right, Elton. You totally saw right through my post."

Just then, Izzy came storming down the hall. She stopped right in front of where Emma and Elton were standing.

"How could you!" she shouted. "How could you make up such a terrible story about me and post it where everyone could see it?"

"What?" Emma gasped. "I didn't make up anything. That's exactly how it happened."

"Really? So I was this mean, spoiled brat who almost destroyed Harriet's birthday party? That's how you see it?"

Emma didn't know how to answer. That hadn't been her intention in writing the post. She wanted to say that sometimes fights were silly and based on nothing but ridiculous disagreements.

"Do you know why I hated Izzy's Barbie? Because I was jealous! Because my dad had just lost his job and my parents didn't have money to buy me a fancy, expensive Barbie like hers. I begged and they said we couldn't afford it. I was upset because Harriet got the one I wanted, something I would never have. And I was five years old, Emma! Did you have to make me sound like such a monster? Or maybe that's how you really see me?"

"I-I . . . ," Emma stammered. "I didn't know. I thought you were trying to make Harriet feel bad."

"I was the one who felt bad. I felt so awful for

making Harriet cry. I tried all week to make it up to her. And reading your blog brought up those guilty feelings all over again." She marched off, leaving Elton there with his mouth hanging open.

"Wait, so Lizzy is Izzy?" he asked. "I'm confused."

"Ugh," Emma said with a groan. Why was nothing working out the way she wanted it to? Why was everyone twisting and misconstruing her words? As if that wasn't bad enough, she spotted Harriet headed for her next. Even from all the way down the hall, Emma could see how red and flushed her friend's face was. Harriet was livid.

"So I'm a crybaby? With a bad taste in Barbies?" Harriet confronted her. "How could you? How could you write that about me?"

Elton scratched his head. "Wait. You're Hattie?"

Emma wanted to bang her head against her locker. Why was no one getting her point?

"Did you read the whole post? The part about our bond being stronger than Krazy Glue?" she asked her friend.

"For the record," Harriet fumed, "my Barbie's arm was never the same after you ripped it out. She couldn't move her shoulder anymore and it was really hard to dress her."

"I said you had a big heart," Emma protested. "I said how much your friendship means to me."

"You said I burst into tears and acted like an idiot at my own party!" Harriet seethed. "Honestly, Emma. How could you bring this up all over again when you know how humiliated I was?"

"I'll take it down. I'll delete the post!"

"Why? Everyone's read it." Harriet turned to Elton. "Did you read it?"

Elton nodded. "Yeah, and I told Emma I forgive her."

"Well, I'm glad you do," Harriet replied. "Because I don't. I can't. I never will! Not after this. And you told the world I keep Barbies in my basement? I'm going to be the laughingstock of Austen Middle!"

"But I didn't use your real name," Emma tried to calm her friend down.

"Do you believe everyone in school is stupid? They know you're my BFF. Or you *were*—before you destroyed my life!"

Harriet ran off to the bathroom in tears . . . again.

Elton bit his lip. "You know, you should probably delete what you wrote," he told Emma. "I appreciate the apology, but your post seems to be freaking people out."

Emma slammed her locker and headed straight for Ms. Bates's office. She had to at least settle the Student Congress situation—or all of this would be for nothing.

Ms. Bates was about to take a bite of her morning bagel when Emma barged in.

"So, it's been forty-eight hours now," Emma said. "My life is a wreck. Can I please go to DC?"

"Why is your life a wreck?" Ms. Bates gestured to a seat across her desk and Emma flopped down into it.

"Everyone hates me—except Elton. He forgives

me. I'm not sure what I did to him, but he forgives me."

"Who's everyone?" Ms. Bates took a sip of tea. "That may be a bit of an exaggeration."

"No. It's not. Everyone who matters in my life hates me—or thinks I'm nuts. Harriet, Izzy, Jax."

"I beg to differ. Jackson made a very heartfelt plea on your behalf yesterday. He wanted you to take his place on Student Congress."

"And I heard you said no."

"I said yes," Ms. Bates replied. "But then I told him how amazing an opportunity this would be and he reconsidered."

"He did *what*?" Emma gasped. She tried to wrap her brain around the fact that for all intents and purposes, Jackson had lied to her face. He had reconsidered his decision to give her his spot. And here she thought he was being kind and selfless!

"So, now you'll have a friend along for the ride," Ms. Bates said.

"What do you mean?" Emma asked cautiously.

"I mean you upheld your end of the bargain, so I will uphold mine. I've decided Austen Middle will be sending you as the second representative to the National Student Congress in two weeks. You beat out a lot of other students who were very qualified, and you proved yourself to me. Congratulations, Emma."

Ms. Bates extended her hand to shake Emma's across the desk, but Emma was too stunned to respond.

"Did you hear me? You're going to DC," the principal repeated. "As a member of the National Student Congress. Isn't that what you wanted?"

Emma nodded. It was what she wanted. But it also didn't feel as great as she had thought it would. Her BFFs were furious with her; Jackson had been dishonest. Those two details kept overshadowing the joy she thought would come from this victory.

"Well, I have morning announcements to make," Ms. Bates said, trying to shoo Emma out of the office. "Your appointment to the Congress being one of them. Run along, Emma."

Emma obeyed and closed the door behind her. Why did this moment feel like such a letdown? Why did her heart feel so heavy and empty at the same time? Why were everybody else's problems easy to solve . . . but not her own?

7

A ROYAL PROBLEM

Mr. Carter, Jackson's history teacher, was the official coach for Student Congress—and he took his job very seriously. He insisted that Emma and Jackson stay after school three days a week to research and write their arguments.

"The goal is to be the expert on the topic you are given so you can persuade the panel of judges to agree with you," Mr. Carter explained. "You have to present a convincing argument."

Emma knew a thing or two about how to state her opinion convincingly, but she wasn't thrilled that she had to work as a team with Jackson—especially knowing that he had lied to her.

"I didn't lie," he tried to explain. "You didn't give me a chance to tell you what happened."

"You said you gave up your spot for me," Emma reminded him.

"I did! I marched in there and told Ms. Bates I was handing it off to you. Then she said I would be crazy to not go—this was the chance of a lifetime—and she was pretty sure you were going to be earning your own spot."

"But you didn't know that for certain. As far as you knew I was out and you were in."

"Emma," Jackson said, "I really wanted you to do this. And I still do. I think we're a great team."

Emma felt her cheeks flush and her anger dissipating. "You do?"

"The Dream Team," Jackson replied. "With my knowledge of government and your way with words, how could we lose?"

"The Dream Team," Emma repeated dreamily.

Mr. Carter piled a stack of books on the desks in front of them. "This should get you started."

"What is this?" Emma asked, examining the book covers. *"Biology? The Science of Nutrition?* This doesn't sound like government to me."

"It's your topic, the one Student Congress has assigned you," Mr. Carter said. "You are tasked with arguing why middle schools should support physical education programs."

"PE?" Emma asked. "That's the one class everyone at Austen hates." Then she thought to herself, *Harriet especially*, and remembered how her friend always seemed to fumble the ball or trip over her own two feet running. The image made Emma chuckle, but then she recalled how Harriet hated her more than gym class these days.

"She's right. Even the jocks say it's a bore,"

Jackson added. "You'd think they could come up with a more exciting way to get kids to exercise."

"Then find a solution," Mr. Carter insisted. "You need to convince a panel of teachers as well as your peers that PE is something all kids need in schools— and do so enthusiastically."

Emma nodded. "Enthusiasm is my specialty."

"So I've heard," Mr. Carter sniffed. "Ms. Bates warned me. Just back it up with solid facts or your words will be empty."

The next few days, as Emma struggled to juggle her research for Student Congress with schoolwork, tennis practice, chorus, and all her other responsibilities, she felt stressed to the breaking point, and she needed her friends to vent to. But Harriet and Izzy walked past her in the hallways as if she were invisible. It felt exactly like the Birthday Barbie blowup all over again. She had tried everything she could think of:

leaving Post-it notes on Izzy's locker; offering Harriet her favorite flavor of gummy bears; sending them both ecards. But they were determined to ignore her efforts and hold a grudge. She didn't know how to get through to them. Emma had practically given up, until one lunch period when Lyla rushed into the cafeteria and sat down next to Emma at her empty table in tears.

"So you know how Jordie believes she's royalty?" Lyla asked, sniffling.

"Um, I guess," Emma said. The truth was, she knew exactly what Lyla meant. Jordana Fairfax was not only captain of the cheer squad but also Austen's resident queen bee. Lyla was Jordie's BFF and also one of her minions. Clearly something was very wrong between them.

"I wrote to *Ask Emma* but you didn't answer!" Lyla continued. "This is a desperate situation."

Emma felt awful—she'd been so busy that she hadn't checked her inbox yesterday. "I'm so sorry, Lyla. Please tell me your problem."

Lyla's lip began to tremble. "Jordie was saying that she thought Kate Middleton was more stylish than Meghan Markle, and I said no way, I thought Meghan was stunning with a much better fashion sense—"

Emma held up her hand to stop her. "You're fighting over princesses?"

Lyla nodded. "It's terrible! Lyla won't talk to me! She called me a nincompoop, and I don't even know what that is."

Emma tried not to laugh—but this fight was pretty silly. Lyla grabbed her arm. "I need your help. You have to fix this! Jordie hates me!"

Emma considered. "Okay. Let me figure out the best approach, and I'll post my advice for you tonight."

Lyla heaved a sigh of relief. "Thanks, Emma. You're not as annoying as Jordie says you are. You're kinda nice."

"Thanks," Emma replied. "I think."

So Emma wasn't the only one locked in a feud

with a friend. Somehow Lyla's fight with Jordie, as ridiculous as it seemed, made Emma feel a little better about her own rift with Izzy and Harriet. Maybe this was something that all friends went through. Her mom certainly thought so.

"It's growing pains," her mom advised.

Emma was helping her fold laundry in between choir practice and homework that night, and her mom had asked why she hadn't seen Izzy and Harriet around the house lately.

"All friendships go through them," her mom continued. "You girls are growing up. Your interests change, you start thinking and feeling differently about the world around you. Sometimes that takes a toll on a friendship."

"But what if this is it? What if they never speak to me again? What if everything we had is over, done, finito?"

"I don't think you girls are finito," her mom insisted. "They'll come around. You have to be a little patient."

"I have been patient," Emma said. "It's like they refuse to hear me."

"Maybe you're saying one thing and they're hearing another," Mrs. Woods suggested. "Signals can get crossed."

Emma buried her head in a fluffy towel. "They think I don't care about them. It's ridiculous. As ridiculous as Lyla and Jordie fighting over which princess is more stylish."

"Oh, I love Tiana," her mom said. "She's my favorite. I love that big green ball gown she wears."

Emma giggled. "No, Mom, not Disney princesses. British royalty!"

"In that case, Princess Di gets my vote. My fave monarch by far."

"She's not one of the choices. Lyla likes Meghan and Jordie likes Kate."

"And I like Di. What's wrong with that?"

"Nothing," Emma said, shrugging. "Except that Jordie hates when anyone doesn't agree with her. If she says black and you say white, she sees red."

Emma's fingertips suddenly began to tingle. "Mom! That's it! You just gave me my *Ask Emma* answer." She threw her arms around her mother and hugged her.

"I did?" Mrs. Woods called, as Emma raced upstairs to start writing. "But what about the rest of the laundry?"

"Later!" Emma replied. "I've got a blog to write!"

8

PICTURE THIS

Emma read over the letter Lyla had sent *Ask Emma*: "I didn't mean to hurt my friend's feelings. I was stating my opinion." That, in Emma's opinion, was the true source of Lyla's tiff with Jordie. It had little to do with princesses, and more to do with Lyla asserting herself. Jordie didn't like anyone challenging her.

Emma began to type:

Sit down and talk to your friend and make it clear that your friendship is more important than whatever you are fighting about. But also let her know that you have a voice and she should hear you out, even if she disagrees. Always stay true to yourself. If your friend is a true friend, she will respect you.

The next day, Lyla found Emma in the cafeteria at lunchtime. "I did exactly what you said," she told Emma. "I sat Jordie down at cheer practice early this morning. I told her how important our friendship is, more than any silly argument."

"And?" Emma asked anxiously.

"And she said, 'Fine—just take it back.'"

"Take what back?"

Lyla shrugged. "She wants me to say I was wrong and she was right."

"Oh," Emma replied. "Did you?"

"No," Lyla said. "But I thought about it. Wouldn't it be easier to let her win?"

Emma considered for a moment. "It would, but you have to stand your ground," she insisted. "Go tell her you can't change your opinions but would like to bury the hatchet."

"Bury the what?" Lyla asked, scratching her head.

"It's a figure of speech. It means put your differences behind you."

Lyla nodded. "Okay. I'll try again."

Emma watched as Lyla approached Jordie's table and tapped her friend on the shoulder. She saw Lyla talking, gesturing with her hands, and smiling nervously. Then she saw Jordie get up, turn her back on Lyla, and snap her fingers. The rest of the cheerleaders leaped to their feet and followed Jordie out of the cafeteria.

Lyla shook her head and motioned for Emma to come over.

"I tried to bury the hatchet," Lyla told her. "But Jordie wouldn't hear of it. She said unless I admit Kate is great, I am off the cheer squad. She's gonna kick me off! She can't do that, can she?"

Now Emma was angry. Jordie was captain of the cheerleaders, but she could not simply boot someone off the team for disagreeing with her! This was getting ridiculous—almost as ridiculous as Izzy and Harriet's argument with her. Emma didn't know how to fix her problems, but she could help Lyla. "That's it," she said, tugging Lyla to her feet. "Let's go talk to Coach Hawkins."

They found the coach sitting on the bleachers in the gymnasium, sipping a bottle of green juice.

"So Jordie insists that her princess is more stylish and won't forgive me unless I take it back," Lyla explained. "But I'm Team Meghan on this."

"Let me get this straight," Coach said. "Jordie believes she's right and you're wrong?"

"Uh-huh," Lyla said, nodding.

"And if you won't admit you're wrong, she wants you off the cheerleading team?"

"Yes!" Emma jumped in. "Crazy, right?"

"Not so crazy," Coach Hawkins replied. "You can't have dissension in the ranks."

Lyla looked frantic. "Speak English!" she pleaded.

"Jordana is head cheerleader, and that does grant her a senior position and the respect that comes with it."

"So I have to take it back?" Lyla groaned.

"Not so fast," the coach interrupted. "I suggest we settle this in a show of good sportsmanship."

"Meaning?" Lyla asked.

"Meaning a face-off. On the basketball court, the tennis court, the track—you two decide. Winner gets to have her opinion stand as the victor."

Emma tapped a finger to her lips. "I get what you're saying, Coach, but I may have a better face-off idea . . ."

The next day at cheer practice, Jordana begrudgingly showed up ready to battle Lyla—but not in sports.

"Did you bring your evidence?" Emma asked Jordie.

"This is so ridiculous," Jordie complained—then she saw Coach Hawkins taking a seat on the bleachers. "But yeah, I made the poster."

She unrolled a large oaktag covered with photos of Kate Middleton clipped from magazines. Lyla had done the same for Meghan Markle. The rest of the cheerleaders took their seats next to the coach.

"All right," Emma said. "Let the royal fashion face-off begin! Once Jordie and Lyla have presented, we will vote on the winner."

Lyla volunteered to go first. "Okay, so first look at the white coat she wore for her official engagement announcement," she said. "It sold out in minutes! Everything she wears sets off a huge shopping frenzy."

"Well, same goes for Kate," Jordie said, pointing to her royal's beige platform pumps. "Everyone wanted to wear these after she did."

"How do you compare boring beige pumps to these stunning over-the-knee boots?" Lyla asked, pointing to another photo. "Meghan is a modern princess. She knows how to be chic and trendy and never looks frumpy."

"Kate is not frumpy!" Jordie was starting to sound very defensive. "She's a power dresser. She looks appropriate for every occasion but gives it her own spin."

"Maybe," Lyla said. "But Christmas 2017 was a big fashion don't." She pulled out of her bag a single photo, blown up to show Kate and Meghan walking side by side as they left church. Kate was in a loud plaid double-breasted coat, while Meghan wore a belted camel coat. The cheerleaders and Coach Hawkins all nodded enthusiastically.

"Which would you wear, Jordie?" Lyla asked her, knowing how her friend was anything but mad about plaid. In fact, Jordie hated it. "Didn't you once tell me to go home and change my yellow plaid skirt because it was hurting your eyes?"

"Well, I . . ." Jordie tried to come up with something in her defense. "Fine, Kate was a bit off that one day. She was pregnant so she gets a pass."

"Perhaps we should put it to a vote," Emma

interjected. "Raise your hand if you think Lyla wins the fashion face-off."

Every hand in the gymnasium went up—even Coach Hawkins's. Jordie looked like she was going to explode: Her cheeks were bright red and her lips were tightly set in a snarl. But she couldn't do anything about it—she had been outvoted.

"Well, in studying these photos of Kate and Meghan, I think it's a draw," Lyla said suddenly. "They both have their style strengths and weaknesses. I mean, look at this bizarre brown hat Meghan wore with her Christmas coat. What's that about?"

Jordie's face softened. "So you're saying that Kate did a better job with her accessorizing?"

Lyla nodded. "Yup."

Jordie smiled slyly. "So I win."

"In this example, absolutely," Lyla told her. "Meghan hasn't quite got the whole royal-hat thing down yet. They don't wear a lot of those in Hollywood. Which means we have nothing to fight over. So, can we go back to being friends?"

Jordie seemed appeased. "Fine. We only have ten minutes left for practice. Assemble!"

Emma patted Lyla on the back. "Good job," she said. "You didn't let Jordie push you around."

Lyla shrugged. "I had to find a picture that let us both win. Even if I do think Meghan is a much better dresser..." She winked and raced toward center court to take her spot beside Jordie in the squad formation.

Emma thought Lyla's solution was brilliant. Why hadn't she thought of it? She looked at her watch: It was 3:45. Izzy would be at her gymnastics meet, probably doing her routine on the balance beam, as Harriet sat in the viewing stands, cheering her on. Emma belonged there as well, but Izzy had made it clear: She was not invited. She wished there were a photo she could pull out of her bag to patch things up like Lyla had. Then it occurred to her . . . maybe there was!

9

MONKEYING AROUND

Emma found what she was looking for in one of her mom's old scrapbooks: a photo of Emma, Izzy, and Harriet in kindergarten on the day of the big zoo trip. They were posing in front of the monkey house, Emma grinning, Harriet twirling her hair, and Izzy looking vaguely annoyed. Emma remembered their teacher, Ms. Bhatia, had instructed the class to gather around the monkey exhibit, and Emma wiggled her way into the front row to get a closer look.

"What do you call those?" she asked her teacher. "The big, funny ones?"

"Those are orangutans," Ms. Bhatia told her.

"How do you spell that?"

Emma was always writing things down and taking notes, even in kindergarten. Somehow, it made things stick in her brain when she did, and *curiosity*—as her dad liked to say—should have been her middle name, not Elizabeth.

Emma pulled her composition notebook out of her Dora the Explorer backpack and scribbled the letters Ms. Bhatia dictated.

One of the orangutans got closer to the cage bars as if to see what Emma was busy doing.

"Chester likes you," the tour guide said.

"Chester," Emma repeated. "Can you spell that, please?"

Izzy rolled her eyes. This was taking way too

much time in her opinion, and she wanted to see the sea lions. She thought they were way cuter than the big hairy orangutans.

"Okay, buh-bye, Chester," she said, tugging on Emma's arm.

"Let go." Emma pulled back. "I need to write down his name."

"You're always writing stuff down," Izzy complained. She tugged again, and this time the pencil went flying out of Emma's hand and rolled inside the cage where Chester dutifully picked it up. He examined the tip and the eraser; he used it to scratch behind his ears; he waved it in the air like a magic wand. The entire class laughed and applauded, except Emma, who was now pencil-less.

"Can he write?" Emma asked the tour guide.

"Not like you can," the guide explained. "He wouldn't know what the letters meant. But he could probably mimic the motions. Orangutans have very strong hands and can manipulate lots of different tools."

"But he couldn't write me a note, like, telling me what he was thinking?" Emma continued.

"He's thinking, can you please go away and leave me alone?" Izzy muttered under her breath.

"No, he doesn't speak our language," the guide explained, "although some orangutans are very smart and have been known to repeat human words."

Emma looked deep into Chester's eyes. "He can't write what he's thinking," she repeated. "That's sad."

Izzy had just about had it. She was afraid they would have to head back to the school bus without seeing the sea lions! "Can we go, Ms. Bhatia?" she begged. "This is soooo boring! Right, Harriet?" She elbowed her friend for backup.

"The monkeys are funny," Harriet said. Izzy gave her a dirty look and she added, "But the sea lions are funny too."

Emma had to leave Chester and her favorite pencil behind. The sea lions were fine, but all they could do was clap their flippers and dive under the water for fish. She glanced back over her shoulder at the monkey house where Chester was probably wondering where she had gone. Maybe she could teach him how to write his ABCs . . . it wasn't that hard, after all. If only she could go back and see him . . .

"All right, class, time to get in line and head back to school," Ms. Bhatia announced.

The kindergartners dutifully lined up in pairs—except Izzy. Her buddy was missing.

"Emma's not here," she reported to Ms. Bhatia.

"What? Are you sure?" Their teacher counted the students over and over, and one was definitely missing.

"Did you see where she went? Did she go to the bathroom? To get a balloon?" Ms. Bhatia asked, practically shaking Izzy by the shoulders.

"Nope," Izzy replied. "I didn't see. I was waving to the sea lions."

Elton raised his hand. "I saw where she went, Ms. Bhatia," he volunteered. He pointed to the monkey house. "She went that way."

With that, the students linked hands and raced toward the monkey exhibit with Ms. Bhatia leading the way. There, seated cross-legged on the floor outside the cage, was Emma. She was carefully writing the letters the guide had told her, C-H-E-S-T-E-R, in her notebook.

"Emma!" Ms. Bhatia shouted. "You scared us! We thought we'd lost you!"

"I was right here; I wasn't lost," Emma insisted. "And look! Chester gave me back my pencil."

"Gave it back?" Ms. Bhatia gasped. "How?"

"He rolled it right under the bars. He must have known it was my very favorite pencil with the purple eraser on it."

Ms. Bhatia couldn't believe what she was hearing, but the pencil was back in Emma's possession.

"Okay, everyone. We've had enough excitement for the day. Time to go back to school." She counted over and over to make sure everyone was with their buddy and made Izzy promise not to let go of Emma's hand until they were safely seated back on the bus.

"You made friends with a monkey," Izzy teased as they walked toward the exit.

"An orangutan," Emma repeated. "O-R-A-N-G-U-T-A-N. Orangutans make very good friends."

"But I'm your friend," Izzy said. "Your best friend."

"You made me lose my pencil, and Chester gave it back. Maybe he's a better friend than you are."

Tears welled up in Izzy's eyes, and she stopped walking. "You don't want to be my friend anymore?"

"Oh, I do!" Emma exclaimed. She hugged Izzy tight—she hadn't meant to hurt her feelings and make her cry. "I know you didn't mean it. We're friends forever. And ever. And happily ever after, to the moon and back." That was the longest amount of time Emma could imagine.

"Okay," Izzy said, sniffling.

They walked silently back to the bus holding hands tightly and didn't say another word about the zoo trip. But for years, Izzy loved to tease Emma about her "orangutan encounter" and how Emma had allowed her curiosity to get her lost in the monkey house. "Classic Emma, classic Emma!" Izzy taunted her.

Emma took the photo out of the scrapbook and scanned it into her computer. She began a new post:

> Sometimes, pictures speak louder than words. I could talk and talk and write and write and I can't seem to get my point across. So here's a picture that I hope explains everything I'm feeling and will always feel.

When Emma walked into school on Monday, she refused to get her hopes up. The last post she'd written for Izzy and Harriet hadn't worked, and she wasn't sure this one would. But at lunchtime, she noticed her friends making their way toward her table with their trays.

"Where'd you find that picture?" Izzy asked her tentatively.

Emma gulped. Did this mean her friend was talking to her again?

"In one of my mom's old scrapbooks," Emma replied.

"I was missing my front tooth in that picture," Harriet chimed in.

Emma braced herself. Was Harriet about to scold her for posting a horrible photo of her on her blog?

Instead, Harriet laughed. "OMG, it was the first tooth I lost. I swallowed it eating one of your mom's walnut brownies the day before. Remember? She felt so bad she gave me twenty dollars and said the tooth fairy gave it to her to pass along?"

"Really?" Emma replied nervously. "The tooth fairy only gave me one dollar for my first tooth."

"You didn't swallow yours," Harriet pointed out. "It fell out when you bit into that candy apple on Halloween."

"Oh." Emma nodded. She could feel the tension between them floating there, heavy, in the air. "So, did you like the post?" She looked at Izzy, trying to get a read on her.

"Here," Izzy said, shoving a folded piece of paper across the table toward her. Emma opened it. It was a sheet of composition notebook paper, and on it, written in childish handwriting, were the words: "HAPILE EVA AFTA TO THE MOON AND BACK."

"You never could spell," Izzy said with a chuckle. "But you always could write. You gave this to me on our bus ride home from the zoo."

"You kept it all this time?" Emma asked.

"In my jewelry box with the lock and key," Izzy said, shrugging. "The one where I keep the stuff that matters to me the most."

Harriet nodded. "She has the love letter that Ben wrote to her in it."

Izzy shot her a look. "Yeah, well, I should probably go through it and toss some stuff out." She paused. "But not this. This means a lot to me."

"It does?" Emma asked hopefully.

"Maybe we were a little harsh . . . ," Izzy continued.

"Maybe we overreacted a tad."

A tad? The past several days had felt like torture! Emma took a deep breath and remembered that she was guilty of overreacting sometimes as well. "I shouldn't have turned my back on you guys. Even if I made that promise to Ms. Bates, your friendship means more to me than any Student Congress."

"Elton said you're going," Harriet piped up. "And you and Jax are working *together*."

Emma blushed. "We are. And I wanted so badly to tell you both all about it! I had no one to talk to!"

"Well, we're listening," Izzy said. "Spill."

"Our topic is whether schools should have physical education programs. At first, I wasn't excited about it, but Jax and I have been doing all this research together. He's so good at finding the facts, and then I write down the points and how we'll argue them."

Harriet looked confused. "So you're arguing? Isn't that *not* a good thing when you're trying to get someone to be your boyfriend? I know I hate whenever Marty and I don't see eye to eye. Just last week he said he thought *Black Panther* was the best superhero movie ever made and I said, 'No way! *Wonder Woman* is way better.'"

"And then you kissed and made up?" Izzy teased.

Harriet blushed. "No, but he invited me over to his house to watch *Guardians of the Galaxy* and I forgave him."

"Jax and I aren't arguing," Emma assured her friends. "We're building an argument to present to the Congress *together*. Jax said we're 'the Dream Team.'"

Izzy raised an eyebrow. "Well, that sounds promising!" For the rest of the lunch period, they gossiped and giggled just like old times, as if nothing had ever come between them. Emma felt like a huge weight had been lifted. The three amigos were back!

"I missed this. I missed you," she blurted out suddenly.

"Me too!" Harriet said, throwing her arms around her friend. "It's not the same without Emma in our lives."

Izzy nodded. "You definitely make things more

interesting," she admitted. "For the record, I missed you too. And you would not believe what happened at the gymnastics meet! Classic Harriet."

"Harriet, you didn't distract Izzy . . . did you?" Emma asked gently.

"No! She won!" Harriet said, sounding a bit defensive.

"And then . . . ," Izzy prodded her.

"And then I got so excited I jumped up and down and fell off the bleachers." She held out her leg under the table to reveal a bandage wrapped around her ankle. "I sprained it," Harriet said.

Izzy couldn't stop herself from laughing. "She went *splat* right on the gymnasium floor. Luckily, there were mats down."

"Oh, Harriet," Emma said, patting her friend on the back.

"I know. I probably need to be a little less enthusiastic. But I couldn't help it. Izzy took home the gold medal and she's going to states!"

"You are? That's so amazing! Congratulations!"

Emma said. "When are they?"

"Two weeks," Izzy said, beaming. "You'll *both* come, right?"

"Absolutely!" Emma exclaimed. Then she remembered what was happening in two weeks. "Wait, is it the weekend of the fifteenth?"

"Yup!" Izzy said. "Put it on your calendar with a big red circle around the date."

Emma didn't know how to tell her: A big red circle was already around that date on her calendar. It was the weekend of Student Congress in DC.

"Why don't you look happy?" Harriet asked.

"I-I can't make it. It's the weekend of Student Congress."

"Oh," Harriet said softly.

Emma looked at Izzy, trying to gauge her disappointment. Just when they were back to getting along great . . .

"I understand," Izzy said.

"You do?" Harriet asked. "Did you hear her? She can't come?"

"I would never tell you to miss the Congress," Izzy replied. "That would be selfish. Like pulling you away from the monkey house to see the sea lions." She smiled. "It's okay, Em. Really. But I want details when you get back. Especially Jax details."

Emma breathed a sigh of relief. "I'll tell you everything, I promise. If we get past the first rounds Saturday, we go to the finals Sunday. But there's so many teams of students competing from around the country, who knows."

Izzy reached across the table to squeeze her hand. "You're going to win. You're Emma."

Emma smiled. "You too. You're Izzy. And I'm going to count on Harriet to video every second of your routine—and you winning that gold medal."

"Just try not to sprain the other ankle when you do," Izzy warned Harriet.

The three of them laughed till their cheeks hurt. Emma wished she could have snapped a photo of this moment to keep in a scrapbook too—but Ms. Bates forbid anyone from using their cell phones at lunch.

"Take this," Izzy offered, handing Emma the note she had kept safe all these years. "For luck at the Student Congress, and to remind you we're there with you in spirit." She held it in the air for a second. "Keep it safe because it's really special to me."

"I will," Emma said, smiling. "And you guys are really special to me."

10

BIG-DAY BUTTERFLIES

Over the next two weeks, Jackson and Emma spent every spare moment they had going over their research and rehearsing their arguments. Before they knew it, they were on the train to Washington.

There would be three rounds: Emma would take the first, Jackson the second, then she would close with the third. For each point they made, the opposing team would have the opportunity to argue their points: why PE *wasn't* needed in schools. This was the con, or against, argument, while theirs was pro, or for. Each round lasted a mere three minutes— so the participants had to speak concisely, clearly, and get the most important and convincing facts across.

"Don't forget to say the part about how physical exercise relieves tension and anxiety—that's key," Jackson reminded her on the train ride to DC. "Students have a lot of stress."

"You're giving me a lot of stress," Emma said. "I know, Jax. We've been over this ten times."

"I want to make sure we stick to the points," he said, waving an index card in her face. Representatives were only allowed to jot notes on small cards. "We have a lot of statistics to incorporate and sometimes you wander off topic."

"Me?" Emma exclaimed. "I do not!"

"You do. You get really excited about something and you burn through those three minutes without mentioning all the statistics."

"Try me. Three minutes on the clock. Now."

"You're on!" Jackson hit the stopwatch on his phone and Emma began to recite: "According to the American Psychological Association, fifty-three percent of teens say they feel good about themselves after exercising, forty percent say exercise puts them in a good mood, and thirty-two percent say they feel less stressed after exercising." She made sure she mentioned all the points on her index card labeled *Stress* and finished just as Jackson called time.

"See? I've got this," Emma declared. "And I have my cards color-coded for each argument. Red for *Stress*, yellow for *Long-Term Health Benefits*, purple for *Learning to Socialize and Work Together*." She started to place the notecards neatly back in their box.

"She's got this," said a voice. Mr. Carter was seated behind them. "You both do. As long as you focus and stick to the points on the cards, you stand a very good chance of winning."

"Really? You think so?" Emma asked him.

"I do," Mr. Carter replied. "You're a good team."

Emma looked over at Jackson to see if he was blushing like she was. Instead, he was staring out the train window and nervously chewing on his thumbnail.

She elbowed him. "I didn't know this meant so much to you," she said softly.

"I thought it didn't, but it kind of does," Jackson replied. "I want to win."

"Well, so do I," Emma answered.

"Yeah, but you have so much else going for you, Emma. As my dad would say, this will be just another feather in your cap. My dad's a prosecuting attorney. He has a lot of feathers in his cap. Unlike me—"

"You've got a lot going for you too! Like . . ." Emma hesitated. Jackson wasn't really involved in any clubs or teams at Austen Middle. He had friends—Elton and Marty always had lunch with him. But he kept to himself a lot. She suspected his previous school in New York City had a lot to do with it. It had taken him a long time to trust her enough to tell her he had been bullied at his old school, and she suspected there was a lot more he wasn't saying. She had thought he liked to be a man of mystery, but now something occurred to her: Maybe he felt insecure. Maybe he was afraid people would reject him or laugh at him.

"Exactly," Jackson said. "Like what?"

"Jax, you're so smart," Emma said. "You're a whiz at so many subjects it makes my head spin. You can do anything you set your mind to. You could be president one day!"

"President Jackson Knight. That has a nice ring to it." He chuckled to himself.

"I mean it," Emma said, touching his hand. "You're amazing. You're caring and kind and you have a great sense of humor." She left out the part about having blue eyes that turned her legs into Jell-O. She held up an index card. "You have so many great things about you, they wouldn't fit on this card!"

Jackson turned to look at her. There was that Jell-O feeling! "How do you do that?" he asked her.

"Do what?" Emma asked dreamily. He also had the cutest dimples.

"Say the right thing every time to make someone feel better?"

Emma shrugged. "It's a talent, I guess."

"It's *your* talent, Emma," he said. "There's really no one like you."

Their faces were inches apart, and she noticed for the first time that he had a few freckles sprinkled across the bridge of his nose. For one brief second, Emma wanted to lean a little closer. His breath smelled like cinnamon gum and—

"Next stop, Union Station," Mr. Carter's voice boomed, making them both jump in their seats. He had totally ruined the moment.

"Does that mean . . . ?" Emma asked.

"Yup!" Mr. Carter said. "We have arrived in DC!"

There was no time to waste. Mr. Carter checked them into their hotel and sent Emma to her room and Jackson to his to get changed immediately for the

Student Congress opening ceremonies.

"You literally have fifteen minutes," he said, shooing them off. "Dress to impress!"

She carefully laid out her outfit on the bed: a simple black skirt and a red blouse with a bow—"power red" was what Izzy had called it when they spotted it in a shop window at the mall. It showed she meant business!

Jackson met her at the elevator; he was still tying his tie when he suddenly looked up. "Wow, you look . . . ," he began.

Emma tugged at the bow at her neck. "Wrinkled. I look wrinkled. I know. I can't help it; my stuff was squished in my bag."

"I was going to say you look pretty," Jackson continued. "Really pretty. Red is your color."

That was a good thing—because her face now matched the color of her blouse! "Thanks. You look good too." Jackson had chosen a light-blue shirt that made his eyes sparkle.

"Good? Not devastatingly handsome and ready

to kick some Congress butt?" he teased. "Make sure you add those points to my card."

"I will," Emma flirted back. "I'm keeping a list."

They found Mr. Carter waiting for them in the lobby, pacing back and forth. "There are some amazing schools here," he told them. "The competition is fierce. We can't afford to make any mistakes."

He ushered Emma and Jackson into the main ballroom where they were each given a name tag and instructed to take a seat at a numbered table.

"There will be opening remarks, then each team will be asked to stand and introduce themselves to the Congress," he explained.

Jackson gulped. "What are we supposed to say?"

"Just your name, the school you represent, and 'I'm honored to be chosen as a member of the National Student Congress,'" Mr. Carter told him.

Unfortunately, Emma wasn't paying attention. She was too busy looking around the enormous ballroom with its twinkling crystal chandeliers and massive stage.

"Is that where we will present our arguments?" she asked, pointing to the podium at its center.

"I believe so," Mr. Carter said. "But all these tables will be gone and replaced with seats—one thousand of them to be exact."

"A thousand?" Jackson looked like he was getting more anxious by the minute. "That many people are going to be listening?"

Mr. Carter nodded. "And there's also the broadcast on the National Student Congress site, which could be accessed by millions around the world."

Jackson wiped some sweat from his brow with the back of his sleeve. "Okay, you did not mention that before."

"There was no need to. And there is no need to worry about it," Mr. Carter assured them. "You are extremely well prepared."

"Easy for him to say," Jackson whispered to Emma. "Are you seeing this?"

"I am!" Emma responded breathlessly. "It's beautiful—and so huge!"

"Really? Doesn't this freak you out?"

Emma shrugged. "Are you kidding? I get to talk to a thousand people? And be broadcast around the world? It's a dream come true!"

Jackson shook his head. "Okay, I'm glad one of us is happy."

They took their seats at table twenty-eight—next to the teams from Fargo Middle in North Dakota and two from Texas—Essex Middle in Houston and All Plains Day School in Dallas.

"Austen Middle?" a girl with owl-like glasses asked Emma. "Is that in Austin, Texas?"

"Our school is named for the great writer Jane Austen," Emma corrected her. "Austen with an *e*. And we're from New Hope, Pennsylvania."

"Uh-huh," the girl replied. "I don't care much for Austen's work. In my opinion, no one can compare to Charlotte Brontë or Edith Wharton." Then she went back to chatting with her teammate—a bespectacled boy.

"Not the friendliest bunch," Jackson observed.

"They're not here to make friends; they're here to win," Mr. Carter reminded him. "As are you. Save the socializing for the big closing gala. I hear they have some famous band performing—uh, Crimson Five?"

"You mean Maroon 5?" Jackson asked excitedly.

"Yes," their adviser replied. "That's it. Have you heard of them?"

"Heard of them? They're only my favorite group on the planet!" Jackson said. It was the first time Emma had seen him excited since they had left home that morning.

"What's your fave song?" Emma asked him. "Wait! Let me guess. 'Moves Like Jagger'?"

"Nope. Keep guessing," Jackson teased.

"Not now!" Mr. Carter hushed them. The judges from the Congress were taking their places onstage.

"Welcome, students and teachers, to the twelfth annual National Student Congress!" said a gray-haired gentleman wearing a suit and bow tie. "I am Mr. Hartfield, president of the Congress and your head judge for the weekend."

Emma noticed that he didn't so much as crack a smile. He was completely, utterly, unshakably serious.

"Hopefully, you are well apprised of the rules for the weekend, but to clarify . . ." He droned on for twenty more minutes, outlining everything in the student manual that Mr. Carter had already drilled into Emma's and Jackson's heads.

Emma stifled a yawn. "Do you think they'll be serving lunch soon?" Her stomach was rumbling, and she'd already dug into the bread basket on the table.

"Shh!" Mr. Carter said, waving a breadstick at her. "Mr. Hartfield is speaking."

"What time is it?" she whispered to Jackson. "I'm starving."

Jackson checked his watch. "Almost noon."

OMG! Emma grabbed her phone out of her purse. Izzy's meet was starting at twelve! "I have to use the ladies' room," she told Mr. Carter, hurrying out of the ballroom to find a quiet corner to call Harriet.

"How is it?" Emma asked as soon as Harriet

picked up, not even waiting for her friend to say hello. "Is she nervous? Are there a lot of gymnasts competing? Are they all really good?"

"Good, yes, yes, and yes—I think those were all your questions," Harriet said. "She hasn't gone yet. There are maybe five girls before she's up."

"Will you tell her good luck for me?" Emma asked. "I got so busy studying on the train I forgot to text."

"Here," Harriet replied. "You can tell her yourself." She handed the phone to Izzy.

"Hey!" Izzy's voice came on the phone. "I let Harriet sit up front this time so we don't have another *splat* incident." She giggled a little. Her voice sounded cool and collected, and Emma was relieved.

"Good luck, Iz! You got this! I know you do!" Emma exclaimed.

"Really? Because I'm not that sure I do. These girls are really good, Em. They're the best of the best in all of Pennsylvania."

"And you're the bestest," Emma assured her.

"Just do you, okay? Don't worry about anyone else. Be the best Izzy you can be and tune out everything and everyone else."

"Hmm, that sounds like an *Ask Emma* post," Izzy said with a chuckle. "You can't turn it off, can you?"

"Guess not," Emma said, laughing too. "Once an advice blogger, always an advice blogger. But you know what I mean."

"Okay, distract me," Izzy whispered into the phone. "How's Jax? Are you working *really closely* with him?"

"There was a moment on the train . . . ," Emma said. "I could feel his breath on my cheek."

"OMG!" Izzy cried. "Did you kiss?"

"I thought we might. But then Mr. Carter had to jump in and destroy it."

"Do you think Jax likes you? What am I saying? Of course he does! Do you think he'll ask you to be his girlfriend?" Izzy was talking a mile a minute.

"I don't know," Emma said. "He's really nervous about the Congress. He can't really think about anything else. But he did tell me I looked pretty."

"And who told you to wear the red blouse?" Izzy teased.

"You did. Good call."

Suddenly, Emma could hear a lot of noise in the background. At first she thought it was Izzy's meet but then realized it was coming from the hotel ballroom.

"I gotta go—good luck, Iz! I wish I was there to see you win."

"I wish I were there to see Jax's face when you walk into that gala in your dress," Izzy replied. "It's gorge, Em. If he doesn't ask you out after that—"

Emma raced back into the ballroom just as the girl with the glasses from earlier was standing and introducing herself.

"I'm Jessalyn McCutcheon from All Plains Day School in Dallas, Texas. I am deeply honored but not at all surprised to have been chosen to represent my school."

Emma took her seat just as Mr. Carter motioned

her to stand up and give her introduction. She wasn't quite sure what she should say, but she had seen several Miss America contestants on TV introduce themselves . . .

"Hi, my name's Emma Woods from the great commonwealth of Pennsylvania! I love show choir, sushi, and my labradoodle, Jagger. I write an advice blog for Austen Middle School called *Ask Emma*. Got a perplexing problem? A desperate dilemma? I'm your girl!"

Emma sat back down and noticed Mr. Carter's mouth hanging open. He looked horrified.

Jackson stood next. "My name is Jackson Knight from Austen Middle in New Hope, Pennsylvania. I am honored to be representing my school at the National Student Congress." He plunked back down in his chair and looked at Emma.

"That's what you were supposed to say," Mr. Carter scolded her. "Not that you like raw fish!"

"Oh." Emma gulped. "I didn't know."

"Perhaps if you had been paying attention when I

told you earlier," Mr. Carter said huffily.

"It's okay, Emma," Jackson assured her. "Your intro was colorful—like you."

Emma wasn't sure whether that was a compliment or an insult. Was her blouse too loud? She glanced around the table and noticed that the other girls were wearing less exciting navy, black, or beige. Emma certainly did stand out—but hadn't Jackson told her she looked pretty?

"Let's try to maintain a sense of decorum, shall we?" Mr. Carter said. He poked at the salad the waiters had now placed before them on the table. "I know nerves are running high, but we are here to represent Austen Middle. Not win Miss Congeniality."

Emma stared at her salad. She felt as wilted as the lettuce in her bowl. She hadn't meant to say anything embarrassing or inappropriate; she was just being herself. Wasn't that the advice she had given Izzy? To do you?

"We're scheduled to present our arguments at one p.m. in the Taft conference room," Jackson informed her. "Right after lunch." Practically the entire hotel was filled with students who would be debating till only the best and brightest remained.

Jackson picked at the food on his plate. "I can't eat. I'm too nervous."

"You need fuel for your brain," Emma reminded him while secretly hoping he would give her his leftovers. The chicken cordon bleu was so good!

She wasn't feeling jittery at all. She and Jackson were ready, they had their notes organized, and large crowds never scared her. All she had to do was stay calm and stick to the points on her cards.

"Are you going to eat your mashed potatoes?" she asked Jackson. "They're really delicious."

"No. Here." He practically shoved the plate into her lap. "I can't."

"You know what I do when I'm nervous?" Emma said, wiping her mouth with a napkin.

"Talk? You talk a lot, Emma."

"Well, yes. But not just that. I sing show tunes in my head."

Jackson stared at her. "And this helps how?"

"Try to remember a song that lifts you up. For me, it's 'Everything's Coming Up Roses' from *Gypsy*."

"Uh . . . nope," Jackson said. "Don't know that one."

Emma leaned closer and softly sang in his ear. "'*Curtain up! Light the lights! We've got nothing to hit but the heights!*'"

"And this makes you stop feeling nervous?" he asked.

"It does! Just think of a song in your head that makes you happy and confident. Make it your anthem."

Jackson rubbed his temples. "Did I ever tell you that you sound a lot like an advice blog?"

"That's so funny! Izzy said the same thing to me when I called her before."

"I wish I had your confidence, Emma," Jackson admitted. "I know I act cool and like I've got it under control—"

"But inside you're freaking out?" Emma nodded.

"I get it. Everyone feels that way sometimes." She paused. "Am I sounding like an advice blog again?"

"A little, but thanks," Jackson said. "I'll try and sing something from *Grease* in my head."

Emma leaned in. "We go together like *rama lama lama ka dinga da dinga dong*," she sang.

Jackson smiled. "That might do it."

Mr. Carter pushed his plate away from the table. "All right, Team Austen, no more dillydallying. Let's get moving. It's showtime!"

11

GET TO THE POINT

Emma and Jackson took their seats in the Taft conference room and watched from the audience as two other schools battled it out on their topic: "Should school uniforms be required?"

"That's such an easy one!" Emma complained to Jackson. "Uniforms suppress creativity and originality. You can't express yourself if you have to look and dress like everyone else. Your style is a reflection of who you are . . . a mirror into your soul!"

"Great, so we'd win that one. What about *our* topic?" Jackson groaned.

"We'll do fine," Emma said, leaning back in her seat. "These teams aren't so scary."

Just then, she noticed Jessalyn and her classmate staring in their direction. "Why is she giving me the evil eye?" she asked Mr. Carter.

He checked his schedule. "Perhaps because they are your opponents. They're the con side of your argument: The program says Austen Middle versus All Plains Day."

"No way!" Emma said, grabbing the roster out of his hands. Now it was her turn to freak out. How could that snooty girl who hated the greatest female writer of all time be her opponent? Obviously, Jessalyn was trying to shake her confidence—but Emma wouldn't let even a crack about her taste in literature do that!

"It doesn't matter. Stick to your argument. It's rock solid," her adviser instructed her.

The two teams sat back down and now it was Emma and Jackson's turn to take the podium. Jessalyn and her teammate took their seats in the wings, whispering to each other.

"All right, don't forget everything I told you," Mr. Carter said, giving Jackson a slight push toward the stage when Jackson paused a few feet shy of it. "And, Emma, stay on track."

"Oh, I will," Emma said, clutching her box of cards. "They're *so* going down!"

"We now have Austen Middle arguing pro for 'Should physical education be mandatory in schools?' Emma Woods is up first." It was just their team's luck that the head judge was presiding in her conference room! Mr. Hartfield looked so stern and intense, like one of those presidential portraits you see hanging in the Smithsonian.

Emma stood and walked purposefully to the podium. She took out her first index card, glanced at it, then began to speak with confidence and conviction as the large digital clock on the judge's desk ticked down: "Physical education should be mandatory in all middle schools for several important reasons, the first being the stress that exercise can alleviate in a student's daily life . . ." She recounted each of the points on her card, quoting statistics, stressing every single research study, fact and figure, then looked up to see the clock: two minutes, fifty-eight seconds. She'd made it just in time!"

"Thank you, Emma. Jessalyn McCutcheon, your rebuttal please," Mr. Hartfield instructed.

Jessalyn swaggered past Emma and smirked. "Physical education in middle school is a useless and ineffective waste of valuable study time," she began. "Most PE programs lack any exercise benefits, are poorly structured, and fail to even raise a student's heart rate."

"Wow," Jackson whispered to Emma. "She doesn't waste any time, does she? She's tearing our argument to shreds."

"No, she's trying to poke some holes in it," Emma said. "That's okay. Let her. Facts are facts and our argument is stronger and more supported."

When it was Jackson's turn to take the microphone, he took a deep breath. *"Rama lama lama,"* he told Emma. "Here goes nothing."

He looked at his card, then directly at the judges. "Physical education should be mandatory in schools because it contributes to a student's moral development and character. Through PE, students assume leadership positions, cooperate with others, and accept responsibility for their behavior. Several studies have found this to be true . . ." He rattled off each of them, summing up his argument just before the three-minute buzzer sounded.

"Yes!" Emma cheered him from the wings.

Mr. Hartfield was taking diligent notes. "Billy Davis. Your counter," he said. Billy brushed past Jackson and could barely wait to launch into his counterargument. "Physical education encourages hostile behavior and aggression according to a recent medical research study . . ."

Jackson looked at Emma. "Okay, we have to nail

the next one. It's your closing. Go with the long-term health benefits. It's impossible to argue against that."

Emma nodded and waited until Billy was done before she stood. She walked to the podium and reached in her box for the yellow cards with all her points outlined. There were red ones and purple ones, but where were the yellow ones? She looked back at Jackson, panicked.

What's wrong? he mouthed.

She held up the box and shook her head.

"Ms. Woods, are you ready to begin?" Mr. Hartfield asked impatiently.

Emma did the only thing she could think of . . . she sneezed.

"I'm—*ACHOO*—sorry—*ACHOO*—I just—*ACHOO* seem to be having an allergy—*a-a-a-CHOO*—attack."

Mr. Carter raced up to check on her. "Are you all right?" he asked.

"I lost my yellow cards," Emma whispered. "Go with it."

"Oh dear!" Mr. Carter improvised. "I'm afraid my

student is violently allergic to . . . to . . ."

"Roses!" Emma shouted, spying a vase on the judges' table. "*ACHOO! ACHOO! ACHOO!*"

"Well, we will take a small break, remove the flowers from the room, and allow you to regain your composure," Mr. Hartfield said.

"*ACHOO!* Thanks!" Emma said, running out of the room with both Jackson and Mr. Carter trailing behind her.

"What do you mean you lost them?" Mr. Carter asked frantically. "When did you last have them?"

"On the train. Jax and I were talking and . . ." Emma half remembered having the cards in her hands but couldn't recall where they went after that or if she had put them back. She and Jackson had their "moment," then Mr. Carter rushed them to pack up and exit the train.

"Do you remember everything that was on them? We went over it dozens of times," Jackson said. "I'm sure you can do it without the cards."

"I'll try," Emma said.

Mr. Carter looked like he was going to explode. "You will not *try*, you will do it. Now! Before we are disqualified." He stomped back into the ballroom.

"Disqualified?" Emma gasped. She couldn't bear the thought of that happening, of letting Ms. Bates, Mr. Carter, or Jackson down.

"Emma, calm down," Jackson said, putting his hands on her shoulders and gazing deeply into her eyes. "I know you're freaking out, but everyone feels that way sometimes." He paused. "Someone really smart told me that once—maybe some advice blogger?"

Emma smiled slightly. "I wonder who?"

"The point is, you can do this," Jackson continued. "I believe in you."

"Okay," Emma replied. "I got this."

"Of course you do," Jackson said, as he turned her toward the ballroom door and gave her a gentle push. "You're Emma."

Emma walked back inside, taking her spot once again onstage. *Focus*, she told herself. *Stop daydreaming about the missing index cards and Jax's dimples. Focus!*

"Are you all right?" Mr. Hartfield asked her.

"Yes, all better!" she said brightly. "No more sneezes." She wiped her nose with the back of her blouse sleeve for emphasis. "I'm ready."

Over the next two minutes she listed the important points in her argument. She even remembered the complicated medical study that proved "aerobic activity has been shown to increase the size of essential brain structures and the number of neural connections."

The judges were nodding, impressed. Then Emma totally blanked. There was still one minute left on the clock, and she couldn't think of another thing from her cards to say. She saw Mr. Hartfield stifle a yawn. In fact, as Emma glanced around the room, she noticed most of the audience looked so bored they were about to doze off. So she improvised.

"Everyone, up on your feet!" she called. She saw Mr. Carter in the audience, waving frantically at her to stop. Was he trying to signal her "time out!" or communicate in sign language? Still, she kept going. "Do five jumping jacks with me. Right here, right now."

Amazingly, the audience obeyed. Even Mr. Hartfield was on his feet, jumping and waving his arms in the air with a surprisingly big smile on his face.

"Now, think about what you just did," Emma told the crowd. "You're smarter, more energized, more emotionally balanced, happier, and less likely to die of a horrible disease. How awesome is that? Don't you want to do more? Don't you believe PE should be mandatory in schools?"

"Yeah!" a kid cheered from the audience.

"Totally!" said another. "I was falling asleep and that was awesome!"

Soon the entire audience erupted in applause.

Emma looked to the wings to see Billy and Jessalyn staring in disbelief, and Jackson pumping his fists in the air.

Jessalyn made her closing remarks but barely

anyone paid attention. Emma's little show had left a lasting impression.

"You hit it out of the park!" Jackson said. "That was incredible!" He leaned forward and swept her into a hug.

Emma could barely catch her breath from all the excitement—and frankly, the feeling of Jackson's arms around her.

"It was okay, right?" she asked.

"It was more than okay. You won this for us, Em!" Jackson said, beaming.

"No, we definitely did it together," Emma insisted. "Your arguments were really strong—and your pep talk helped me a lot. I think we have a good chance."

"I agree," Mr. Carter said, catching up with them to await the judges' decision. "It was a bit unorthodox, but it truly drove the point home."

They waited more than twenty minutes before Mr. Hartfield finally appeared onstage with the panel's decision. "This was a difficult one," he stated to the crowd. "Both Austen Middle and All Plains

Day made very strong, convincing arguments. But in the end, we decided that one team communicated their evidence in an innovative and indisputable way. Congratulations, Austen Middle."

Emma and Jackson couldn't believe it—they were going to the semifinals tomorrow morning!

Mr. Carter looked pleased but not as ecstatic as they were. "Good job, you two," he told them. "Now the real work begins."

12

ON THE SPOT

Mr. Carter explained that, unlike the first round, there would be no preparation for the semifinals. "Whatever topic they give you, you must use your knowledge and skills to argue it effectively. There is no research to look at this time. You are exhibiting your skills as an effective communicator."

"So, Emma should have this one down," Jackson said, winking at her.

Mr. Carter was not as sure. "The judges will be scoring you not only on how well you argue your point but on how well you listen and respond to what your peers are saying." He shot Emma a serious look. "You cannot get carried away. Every single word counts."

Emma nodded. "No jumping jacks. I get it."

"I hope so," their adviser said. "A calm, cool head will take home the trophy."

"We find out the topic on the spot?" Jackson asked.

"You will have thirty minutes to confer before making your case. You'll also decide at that time who will lead and who will close. If you win the semi-finals, you go to the finals against the top students in the country."

All Emma wanted to do at the moment was go to her room, call Harriet and Izzy, and get a good night's sleep. She was exhausted. But Jackson had a better idea.

"Want to go sneak a peek at my future home?" he asked her.

"Your what?" she asked, confused.

"Don't you remember? President Jackson Knight? I hear there's a student sightseeing tour tonight that includes a stop in front of the White House."

Emma thought hard—she was really tired. But those blue eyes were so convincing. "Okay," she agreed. "Give me a few minutes to check in and see how Izzy did at states. She's not going to believe we won today."

Emma plopped down on a couch in the hotel lobby and called her friend.

Harriet answered on the first ring. "We're watching the debate now on the website. OMG, Emma, you were amazing with that opening argument! Your mom and dad are having everyone over for dinner and a screening. Even Ms. Bates and Jax's parents are here!"

Emma could hear her parents cheering, "Emma! Emma!" in the background. She'd completely forgotten that Mr. Carter mentioned it would be broadcast on the National Student Congress website.

"Honey?" Her mom came on the phone. She must have grabbed it out of Harriet's hand. "You're amazing! We're watching it now. Did you win? Wait, don't tell me. Okay, tell me . . ."

"We're going to the semifinals," Emma said proudly.

"They're going to the semifinals!" Mrs. Woods shouted to her living room packed with guests.

"Whoa, Mom, could you at least issue a spoiler alert?" Emma heard Luc complain. But everyone else was cheering.

Izzy took the phone next. "My friend, the champion," she said. "You know it was the power-red blouse, right?"

"Iz, did you win the gold medal?" Emma asked her anxiously.

"Silver, but it's okay. It means I'm an alternate for nationals in the spring."

Emma could hear disappointment in her voice.

"That's great!" Emma said, trying to be cheerful. "Silver is great!"

"Well, it's second to great, right?" Izzy said.

"Izzy . . ." Emma wanted to say something comforting, something that would make her feel happy. But instead, Emma held herself back and listened.

"I was so close," Izzy said. "I lost by a tenth of a point. Isn't that crazy? But this girl from Pittsburgh was crazy on the parallel bars and I did wobble on my dismount."

"I'm sorry," Emma said. "I know you wanted gold."

"You can't win 'em all, right?"

"I wish I were there, Iz."

"I wish I were there with you, Em. Good luck tomorrow."

Harriet got back on the phone. "Knock 'em dead, okay?" she told Emma. "Your mom made lasagna, so I gotta go. It's getting cold."

As Emma hung up, Jackson walked over. "So?

What did I miss?"

"It sounds like most of Austen Middle, including your parents, are eating lasagna and watching us win on the National Student Congress website," she told him.

"How about Izzy?"

"She came in second. She's trying not to act sad, but I know she is."

"Well, work your Emma magic and say something to make her feel better."

Emma thought for a moment. "I tried. But there's nothing I can really say to fix it."

"And you hate when that happens," Jackson finished her thought.

"More than anything. It makes me feel like a failure."

"You? A failure?" Jackson gasped. "Emma Woods, if there is one thing in the world you will never be, it's a failure. You wouldn't know how."

"Thanks," Emma said, then she gave him a little smile. "I really wish Izzy could have won. It would have made today perfect."

Jackson held out his hand to pull her up from the couch. "Well, the day's not over yet. It might be perfect, if you give it a chance."

Emma and Jackson spent the next few hours taking selfies in front of all the DC monuments and wound up at the gates of the White House. They strolled down Pennsylvania Avenue, trying to find a quiet spot away from the tour group.

"You really suppose I could be president one day?" Jackson asked her.

"Why not?" Emma said, taking a bite out of a hot dog from a street cart.

"Maybe a congressman," Jackson pondered. "That's probably more doable."

"I say, reach for the moon," she said. "If you fall, you land among the stars."

"Did you write that?"

"No," Emma said, giggling. "It's on this mug that Luc gave me for Christmas. But I always liked it."

The final stop on the tour was the Washington Monument—which Emma cheerfully pointed out resembled a giant pencil.

"You really are a writer," he teased her. "It's all you think about."

"No," Emma insisted. "Sometimes I think about other stuff." What she wanted to say was *I think about you, Jax, all the time!* But instead, she kept silent and watched the sunset over the monument.

"So, if there are no stars out, can you make a wish on the moon?" Jackson asked her.

"Hmm, that is highly unorthodox," Emma said, doing her best Mr. Carter impression. "But go for it!"

"I wish—" Jackson began but Emma covered his mouth with her hand.

"No!" She hushed him. "Never tell anyone your wish or it won't come true."

"Says who?" Jackson asked.

"I'm not sure."

"Stick to facts, Ms. Woods," Jackson said, imitating

Mr. Carter. "If you have no supporting evidence, I'm wishing out loud."

"Okay," Emma said, giggling.

"I wish that we win Student Congress tomorrow," Jackson said.

Emma thought it was a good wish, given their circumstances, but she had hoped he would wish for something a little more personal—like her becoming his girlfriend.

"Your turn." He elbowed her.

"I'm going to keep mine a secret," she insisted. "Just in case that works better."

She closed her eyes and made her wish silently: *I wish that tomorrow is the most perfect day of my entire life.* She thought that covered all the bases.

Jackson saw that the tour guide was motioning for them to board the bus back to the hotel. "Aw, I wish we had more time to hang out," he said.

"That's your second wish," she teased. "There is a limit." But she felt the same. Today had been amazing from start to finish, and she hated to see it end.

13
ROUND TWO

Bright and early the next morning, Emma and Jackson met Mr. Carter in the hotel restaurant to have breakfast together. She ordered a hearty omelet, toast, and bacon, while Jackson pushed around his bowl of cereal, and their coach downed cups of black coffee.

"I hope you both slept well," he told them, mopping his brow with a napkin. Emma thought he looked more nervous than Jackson. "I was up all night and didn't sleep a wink. I made a chart of the teams that are in the semifinals, ranking the ones I believe are our most serious competition." He handed Emma the list.

"Columbus Prep is the one to beat, huh?" she asked, looking it over.

Jackson grabbed the paper out of her hands. "Columbus Prep? From New York City?"

"Yes," Mr. Carter said. "They've won twice in past years. Have you heard of them?"

Jackson gulped. "I went to school there."

Emma knew what that meant. This was the school where Jackson had been bullied. This was the school that he'd left to come to Austen this year. This was the one school he wanted to forget.

"It's okay, Jax," she said.

"I know," he said, trying to act nonchalant. "I'm okay. It was a surprise, that's all."

"Great," Emma said, crossing her fingers that Jackson was truly not worried about facing his former classmates. He was stressed enough; this was the last thing he needed.

They walked into the ballroom where the stage was now set up for the semifinals. Rows of chairs were lined up behind the podium for the students to take their spots.

"Do you see the Columbus Prep kids?" she whispered to Jackson.

He looked around the room. It was filling up quickly with students, coaches, and spectators. "Not yet. But I'm not going to think about it. I'll focus on what we need to do."

"Good idea," she said. "We will both think of nothing besides the competition." Then she noticed the media pouring into the room. "Would you look at all these reporters? And cameras!" Emma said, smoothing her hair and making sure her shirt—a purple silk button-down that Izzy had also helped her pick out—was tucked neatly into her skirt.

"I'm trying not to look," Jackson replied, shielding his eyes.

"But it's so cool," Emma tried to convince him. She waved into a camera lens that was panning the room. "The whole world could be watching!"

It took Jackson several minutes to pry Emma away from the media so they could take their seats in the second row of the stage next to a pair of students from Eagle Eye Middle in Indiana and a duo from Alameda Academy in California. In all, there were about thirty schools remaining, and by the finals there would be only six. The judges would then rank them and award one grand prize.

On Emma's seat was an envelope that they were not to open until the judges started the clock. In it was the topic they would be debating, and their assigned position—either pro or con.

"I have a good feeling about this," she told Jackson, holding the envelope between her palms. Her fingertips got that familiar tingly feeling—the one that always told her she was on the right track. "It's going to be a really good topic, and we'll rock it."

Jackson kept his head down, staring at his shoes.

"Jax, you okay?" Emma asked him gently. She noticed he looked a little pale. "You don't look so good."

"I'm fine," he said, trying to convince both of them. "I'm trying to save my energy."

Mr. Hartfield called the room to attention. "When I sound the bell, you will have exactly thirty minutes to prepare your arguments." Emma held the envelope in her hand, poised to tear into it. "On your mark, get set . . . ," the judge announced. "Open your envelopes!"

Emma ripped hers open and pulled out the card inside.

"What does it say? What did we get?" Jackson asked anxiously.

"Homework should be mandatory in schools: PRO," she read aloud.

Emma looked at Jackson. "Pro? We're supposed to argue that homework is a good thing? When every student on the planet—including me—hates it?" she exclaimed. Now it was her turn to freak out.

"We can't think like that." Jackson tried to rein her

in. "We have to defend our topic, so let's start writing down notes." He pointed out that classes were only forty minutes long—making it difficult to study a subject in depth. Homework also reinforced topics that were covered in class by giving students a chance to practice what they had learned—like when students employed a new formula in math homework.

Emma and Jackson were barely finished scribbling out their talking points when Mr. Hartfield announced the thirty minutes were up. Several other students were up before Austen Middle, which gave Emma just enough time to go over their argument in her head and Jackson more than enough time to continue panicking. They decided that he should open and she should close—summing things up in a neat little package was her specialty. Jackson and one of the Eagle Eye students stepped forward to draw straws—whoever got the shorter one would go first. Jackson took a deep breath and selected his straw—it was the longer of the two, so he could hear his opponent's argument and counter it.

Emma gave him a thumbs-up and listened intently as one of the two boys from Eagle Eye argued that homework prevented kids from having ample time after school to rest their brains, de-stress, and engage in extracurricular activities. All were excellent points that she agreed with! Still, she and Jackson had to prove them wrong.

"My opponent makes good points," Jackson began his speech. "As a student, I'm not a fan of homework either and would rather be shooting hoops. Yet I recognize its value in the learning process . . ."

Emma studied the judges, trying to figure out if Jackson was swaying them to his side, but they were all annoyingly stone-faced. The second Eagle Eye student took the podium and argued against everything Jackson had said: In his opinion, schools should "make periods slightly longer to get in sufficient study time and reinforce the lessons without making kids stay up late with hours and hours of homework. If teachers did their jobs, homework would be unnecessary."

You tell 'em! Emma wished she could shout in response. Everything the boy had said was exactly what she was thinking! She hated when her math teacher gave them complicated examples to wrestle for homework so she had to miss watching the new episode of *The Bachelor*. Or when her chem lab write-up took her practically all weekend and she couldn't hang with Izzy and Harriet at the mall.

"Miss Woods?" Mr. Hartfield's booming voice snapped her out of her trance. "You're up."

Emma took the podium. She looked out at the cameras, all focused on her. In that instant, she knew exactly what it would take to win this round: not more boring facts, but a strong, positive, concrete Emma example!

"So, over holiday break in sixth grade, my family went to visit my Gram Millie and Papa Lou in Boca," she began. "They have this really nice condo overlooking the beach, and I was looking forward to catching up on the latest entertainment news while lying in the sun. I'd picked up my favorite gossip magazines at the airport newsstand, and I had so many questions that needed answering: Were Selena and Bieber back together? Was another Kardashian expecting? Was Zendaya a fashion do or a fashion don't this week? But no! Mrs. Kimmel assigned us each a book of our choosing to read and write a book report about. So much for relaxing on my week off!"

She noticed that Mr. Carter was pulling on what little hair he had on his head, and Jackson was biting his nails. Still, she kept going: "I began reading *Pride and Prejudice* because I loved the miniseries so much, and well, my gram happened to have an old copy on her bookshelf. But the book was all words, no pictures, and it was long—like two hundred and fifty pages long! I wasn't happy at first. In fact, I was really annoyed and thought it was ruining my vacation. But then, Gram sat down with me, and we read some of it together. I got into it: the punchy prose, the unforgettable characters, the relationship between Elizabeth Bennett and Mr. Darcy. It was even better than the movie! I realized what a brilliant writer Jane Austen was and how her stories are really lessons about society and the times she lived in. Her words are smart and always honest; she sheds light on the truth in a way that everyone can understand. I realized on that vacation that I wanted to be a writer too and shed light on truth in my own world of Austen Middle. It planted the seed for me to start my blog, and I have my homework to thank for it. Without this assignment, I would never have discovered my passion or my favorite author. So, in my humble opinion—no disrespect to my opponents, of course—homework is not only necessary, it can change your life for the better. It can help you discover who you really are. Thank you."

She noticed that Mr. Hartfield was writing something down on his notepad as the last few seconds of her time limit ticked down. The rest of the judges continued staring at her blankly—there was no thunderous applause like there had been after her jumping jacks. She glanced back at Jackson, who also looked a bit stunned. Had she been wrong?

Had she made a terrible mistake and cost them the semifinals?

They had to sit through several more debates—including the student representatives from Columbus Prep arguing that students should not be graded on their handwriting—before Mr. Hartfield dismissed everyone for a lunch break. The judges would choose the six teams for the finals and announce them in an hour.

"This is nerve-racking," Mr. Carter said, ringing his hands.

"You can say that again," Jackson replied. If he recognized the kids from his old school, he wasn't telling Emma. In fact, he wasn't saying much. All he whispered when Emma sat back down next to him onstage was "good job," and she didn't quite believe he meant it.

"Are you going to eat that pickle?" she asked, trying to break the ice at their lunch table.

Jackson tossed it on her plate without a word.

"Okay, can we talk about something? Anything?

The weather?" she asked Jackson and Mr. Carter. "The silence is deafening, guys."

"I'm rather enjoying it," their coach said. "Listening to hours of debating has given me a horrible headache."

"Me too," Jackson piped up.

"Okay, fine. I get it. No one wants to talk about how we did. You both believe I totally blew it, and you're wishing Ms. Bates never agreed to send me."

Jackson looked up. "You didn't blow it, Emma. You were great. You spoke from your heart, which is something nobody does quite like you, and if Mr. Hartfield doesn't pick us for the finals, it's his loss."

"Mr. Carter?" Emma asked, eager for his opinion.

"I agree with Jackson," her adviser said. "But I'm not sure the judges will. All we can do now is wait."

14

THE WAITING GAME

Although Mr. Hartfield had promised results in an hour, an hour stretched toward two hours.

"My dad always says 'no news is good news,'" Emma said, trying to cheer up Jackson. He looked as if he were at the end of his rope—and Mr. Carter was doing nothing to help the situation.

"How long can they take?" their coach asked,

loosening his tie. "This is torture!"

Finally, Mr. Hartfield approached the podium and asked everyone in the ballroom to take a seat. "We have the results," he announced. "Thank you for bearing with us. It was a very difficult decision this year."

Emma sat up straight in her seat, crossing her fingers and toes, as Mr. Hartfield read the finalists "in no particular order." He cleared his throat: "Holden Mann Academy, Michigan . . ." A cheer sounded in the room as the two students from the school jumped up and down. "Bayberry Middle from Ohio . . ."

Mr. Hartfield continued, "Mountainview Middle School, Kansas. Benjamin Franklin Middle School, Maryland." He paused and Emma thought her heart was going to leap out of her chest—the suspense was unbearable!

"Columbus Preparatory, New York . . ."

She looked at Jackson. He was shaking his head in disbelief. All around the room, kids were rejoicing, crying, or waiting tensely, hoping for the last spot.

She held her breath waiting to find out which she would be.

Mr. Hartfield looked at his fellow judges, who were nodding approvingly. "And finally, Austen Middle School, Pennsylvania."

"Yaaaaaas!" shouted a voice from the back of the room. "Go, Emma!"

She knew that voice anywhere—it belonged to Harriet. Emma turned to see her friend standing on a chair in the middle of the audience, screaming her head off. Next to her, Izzy, her parents, and Mr. and Mrs. Knight were standing and cheering too.

Emma couldn't tell if Jackson was stunned to see their friends and family in the ballroom or if he was still trying to absorb Mr. Hartfield's announcement. He stood frozen like the Lincoln monument to his spot.

"I don't believe it," he told her finally. "We did it."

"Yeah, no biggie," she teased him.

Harriet was the first one to rush up and congratulate them. "I knew you'd make the finals," she told Emma. "Which is why we decided to drive to DC at the crack of dawn to surprise you. So we could see you kick butt."

"Bravo!" Emma's dad added. "Now we can hear your final argument in person."

Emma noticed that her mom was wiping away tears. "Mom," Emma said. "Really?"

"I'm so proud of you," her mom replied. "We all are."

Jackson looked at his parents. His dad was beaming and his mother was snapping photos of him on her iPhone.

"My future attorney, following in his father's footsteps," his father said, patting Jackson on the back.

"Oh no," Emma piped up. "Jax has much bigger plans than that. He's going to be president one day—just you wait and see."

"President?" Mrs. Knight asked. "Would that make me First Mom?"

"I hate to break up the reunion, but we are wanted

onstage for the final round," Mr. Carter said.

"Gotta run!" Emma said, waving. "We have a Student Congress to win."

Jackson grabbed her arm as they were walking back to the stage. "I have a bad feeling about this," he said. "I think we're going to be up against Columbus Prep." He pointed to a tall girl in a navy turtleneck seated by the podium.

"You know her?" Emma asked.

"She's hard to miss," Jackson replied. "She's the smartest girl in the school and she's only in the seventh grade. Her name's Aubrey Whitehead and she won two state spelling bees, a worldwide Latin contest, and she's president of their student government association. Seriously."

"Whoa." The word tumbled out of Emma's mouth before she could stop it. The last thing she wanted to do was discourage Jackson, but how could they possibly compete with someone that brilliant?

"Well, she doesn't have her own blog—so I'm not that impressed," Emma said.

Jackson rolled his eyes. "If we have to argue against Aubrey, we are doomed, doomed, doomed," he insisted. "She's a walking Google search engine."

"Don't let her intimidate you, Jax," she warned him. "Facts are important, but you've got to have finesse."

Jackson shook his head. "Em, all the finesse in the world couldn't beat Aubrey. But I know you'll try."

"I will," she insisted. "And you will too. No giving up when we've come this far."

Emma and Jackson took their seats, and Emma held the envelope in her hands. "I have a good feeling about this one too," she told her teammate. But her fingertips weren't tingling this time—and it made her a little worried.

"All right, students, open your envelopes," Mr. Hartfield instructed.

Emma tore it open and pulled out the card inside. She read aloud, "Students should have a say in the way their school is run. Austen Middle: PRO; Columbus Prep: CON."

"Doomed"—she heard Jackson muttering under his breath—"doomed."

With only thirty minutes to come up with an argument that would beat the Columbus Prep team, there was no time to waste.

"Oh no," Jackson said, noticing who Aubrey's teammate was.

"Do you know him?" she asked Jackson. "Did he win some worldwide something too?"

Jackson shook his head. "No, worse. That's Tyler Martinez. He's editor in chief of the school newspaper, the *Columbus Prep Pen and Ink*. He's really opinionated, and he writes these 'Letter from the Editor' columns in every issue. He's all about trying to right wrongs and stir things up."

Editor? Column? Opinionated? Right wrongs? Emma was trying to take in everything Jackson said. This Tyler kid sounded, well, a little like her.

"Yeah, he's definitely a guy who writes what's on his mind," Jackson recalled. "Like when they decided to cut back on school library hours. He wrote this long editorial saying how unfair it was and how students should demand their rights to more study time. He said kids should camp out in front of the library doors and refuse to leave until they reopened them for an extra hour. He brought a sleeping bag to school and everything."

"You don't say," Emma replied. Not only was this boy persuasive, he was creative.

"They're going to be impossible to beat." Jackson frowned. "I don't even know where to begin."

Emma took a deep breath and shook off any doubt she was feeling. "I do, we begin at the beginning. What are we trying to say?"

"Students should have a say in their school," Jackson repeated.

"Of course students should have a say in school. It's our lives, isn't it?"

Jackson shook his head. "Not good enough.

Aubrey's going to say that adults know better. And Tyler's going to say schools create rules that are meant to help kids learn and grow and be safe."

"So, how do we fight that?" Emma asked.

"I don't know," Jackson said.

Just then, Emma had a thought. "Well, I do. Ask me a question."

Jackson scratched his head. "What do you mean, 'ask a question'?"

"I mean, I think best when I'm writing an *Ask Emma* post. So ask me! Dear Emma . . ."

Jackson shrugged. "Fine. Dear Emma, my principal wants to make all the rules in school and doesn't want our opinions on anything. It makes me really mad. What can I do to convince her we should have a say?"

Emma grabbed a pen and pad and started writing frantically.

"Tell me you have something," Jackson pleaded with her.

Emma nodded. "Oh, I do."

She tore out a sheet and handed it to him. "This is what you say," she instructed. "Keep it simple and clear. I'll close."

Jackson read it over. "Okay—if you really think this will work."

"It has to," she told him. "Make sure you get the short straw and go first before Aubrey or Tyler has a chance to say anything."

Two of the other teams were up first, tearing each other apart over the topic "Cell phones should be allowed in school."

Emma and Jackson's turn was next.

"Remember," Emma cautioned, as Jackson walked toward the podium. "The shorter straw!"

15

AND THE WINNER IS . . .

As he drew his straw, Jackson closed his eyes and held his breath. When he opened them, he saw that his straw was half the length of Aubrey's.

"Jackson Knight, you are up first," Mr. Hartfield said.

Jackson looked over his shoulder at Emma and mouthed the words, *I got this.* Then he began his speech: "I know what my opponents are going to tell you: Kids can't possibly know what's best for us. How could we? We don't have the life experience that adults do. Our brains are not yet fully developed to help us make crucial decisions. Tweens and teens can be impulsive, insensitive, even selfish—all of which would make for chaos when running a school. So why, you ask, should we have a say?" He paused, as Emma had told him to, to allow the audience to take in what he was saying.

Aubrey looked down at her notes and pouted. Then she whispered in Tyler's ear and he frowned.

Oh, this is too good! Emma thought to herself. Jackson is stealing everything their team planned to say! He beat them to it!

Jackson continued, "Kids should have a say because we need a purpose, a reason to care and to walk through our school doors every day with enthusiasm and pride. Give kids a voice, and we feel respected and heard, and will have a much better attitude and a greater chance at excelling." Mr. Carter gave him a thumbs-up from his seat in the audience, and Jackson concluded with confidence. "Thank you, and I know we all want kids to succeed in school and life."

Aubrey strode up to the podium. "Nice try," she whispered to Jackson as she took the microphone. "I'd like to thank my opponent for so eloquently supporting my side of the argument," she announced to the audience. "He made it so easy for me. Yes, all of what he said is true—except for the part about giving kids a voice being a good idea. It's a terrible idea. Let a kid make the rules, and of course they'll be more inclined to follow them. But what might those rules be? Cell phones at lunch? No homework? 'Fun' classes instead of challenging ones that prepare us for high school and college? It would destroy the entire structure of the education system and the result would be kids who grow into spoiled, undereducated, irresponsible adults."

Jackson and Emma looked at each other. Somehow, Aubrey had overshadowed their argument and managed to get the audience nodding and buzzing.

"This isn't good," Emma whispered.

"You're supposed to be the optimistic one," Jackson said.

"I know," she replied. "But I didn't realize Aubrey was *that* good."

"Oh, she is. I remember when she persuaded the principal to start recycling in the cafeteria. She was relentless."

Emma's eyes lit up. "She did what?"

"You know, recycling?" Jackson tried to explain. "One bin for paper; another for plastic and metal . . ."

"Miss Woods, are you ready?" Mr. Hartfield asked.

"Yup. I'm ready," Emma said, taking her place at the podium. She waited till the judges had started the clock, then turned to face Aubrey.

"Congratulations," she told her, smiling mischievously. "I applaud you." She clapped and watched as Aubrey stared at her, confused.

"You see, my opponent is a perfect example of why students need a voice in how their schools are run. Without her, New York City would have more air and water pollution, more trash in landfills. But she fought hard to start a recycling program in her school cafeteria. So, yay, Aubrey. Good for you!"

Aubrey's jaw dropped. Emma was actually using her accomplishments to shred her argument to bits! And Emma didn't stop there.

"So the administration in Columbus Prep didn't feel a recycling program was a great idea—but they know best, right?" Emma asked the audience. "Well, Aubrey didn't think so. She fought hard as president of her student government to convince her principal that recycling was important. She made a difference, not only in school policy, but in our environment." She pointed to one of the judges who had a paper cup filled with coffee. "You!" she shouted at him. "Do you think you should recycle that cup?"

"Why yes, recycling is very important," the judge responded, embarrassed to be put on the spot.

"It is!" Emma said. "And yet it took a kid to point this out. A kid who couldn't possibly know as much as a grown-up. A kid who is only in the seventh grade but is already concerned with saving our resources and protecting our planet for the future. And that's it, isn't it? Kids are the future. It will be our world one day. The sooner we learn to take responsibility for it, the better the world—and our lives—will be. This Student Congress is the perfect example of how important it is for all of us to have a voice. Isn't that why we're here? To discuss issues, to explore questions, to arrive at answers? Shouldn't every kid, not just the representatives here, have that chance?"

The audience erupted in applause—Harriet leading them by whistling through her teeth.

Emma sat back down and smiled at Jackson. "And that's how it's done."

"That was amazing. You're amazing," Jackson marveled.

"You gave me the idea," she told him. "When you told me about Aubrey being student government president and wanting to recycle."

"Well, that leaves only Tyler," Jackson said. "Let's hope we took some of the air out of his tires."

Tyler had one last argument left to make for the Columbus Prep team. He walked to the podium, cleared his throat, and began. "Yes, Aubrey is student government president, and, yes, she helped implement a recycling program in our school—with the guidance of an adviser, an adult who instructed her and helped her make smart decisions." He turned to Emma and Jackson. "Did you two come here alone?" he asked them. "Or did your adviser work with you tirelessly on your debating skills and prepare you to make the strong arguments you've made today?"

Uh-oh, Emma thought. *This isn't supposed to happen.*

Tyler stepped down off the stage and walked to where Mr. Carter was seated in the audience. "Sir, your Austen Middle students owe you a great deal," he said.

Mr. Carter had no idea what to do—so he tried to hide behind his program.

"Don't be shy," Tyler continued. "Every student here owes a great deal to each of our advisers. Without them, we wouldn't be here today. Our adviser, Mr. Benally, is also my adviser on the student newspaper—he reads all of my editorials before they go to print. Why? Because he's wise and experienced. All of our advisers here today are as well. Many have coached teams to victory at the National Student Congress before. So, yes, kids do have a voice here, but it's because of the expert advice and guidance we've received—proving that as kids, we are not ready to take the reins yet. There will be plenty of time for that."

He then did something completely unexpected— and frankly, Emma-esque. He went around the room, shaking hands with every adviser and thanking them, until Mr. Hartfield called time.

"He out-Emma'd you," Jackson said, shaking his head in disbelief. "That was exactly something you would do."

Jackson was right. It was a brilliant move. If they were playing chess, it would have been checkmate. Tyler had seen Emma's technique and one-upped her. It was unexpected, unorthodox, and the adults in the audience were eating it up.

"Ugh," Emma groaned. "Now what?"

"We wait," Jackson said.

The afternoon seemed to go on forever, with the remaining teams battling it out and the judges deliberating for what felt like an eternity.

No matter how much Izzy and Harriet tried to cheer her up, Emma already felt defeated. She slumped on a couch in the lobby, waiting for the news. Mr. Carter sat down next to her. "Columbus Prep wasn't completely right, you know," he told her. "I guided you, yes, but in the end, you did your own thing, Emma. Your voice is yours and yours alone, and that's the way it should be."

Even with Mr. Carter's pep talk, Emma couldn't help feeling like she'd let everyone down. If her team didn't win, it would be all on her. She was the one who had tried to outmaneuver Columbus Prep. Emma had been overly confident; she never anticipated her opponents beating her at her own game.

She saw Jackson approaching her. "The judges have their decision," he said. "We have to go back in the ballroom."

Emma's heart sank. This was it. Whatever happened next, there was no fixing it.

"Good luck, honey," her mom whispered, as she and Jackson walked past their family and friends in the audience.

"Positive thoughts!" Harriet told her.

Emma couldn't bear to imagine how the Austen Middle fan club would feel if she and Jackson didn't take home the trophy. Her family and friends hadn't come all this way to watch Austen Middle lose!

"Congratulations to each of the schools who made it this far," Mr. Hartfield began. "You are truly all brilliant debaters."

He read off the names of the finalists, one by one, as each team stood and silently marched up to the podium to receive their medals:

"Sixth place: Bayberry Middle School.

"Fifth place: Holden Mann Academy.

"Fourth place: Benjamin Franklin Middle School.

"Third place: Mountainview Middle School . . ."

Emma looked at Jackson and squeezed his hand so tightly, he yelped.

"You know what this means?" she said. "It's us and Columbus Prep."

They were holding hands as Mr. Hartfield read the next name on his list: "In second place, Austen Middle School."

For a minute, Emma felt as if she were having an out-of-body experience. She barely remembered walking up to the podium with Jackson and receiving the second-place medal from Mr. Hartfield. She remembered seeing Harriet, Izzy, Ms. Bates, and their families jumping for joy in the audience, and Mr. Carter waving enthusiastically.

As Emma made her way through the audience, people kept congratulating her. Her parents showered her with praise, bouquets of roses, and congratulations balloons, and Harriet handed her a stuffed orangutan wearing an Austen Middle T-shirt.

"I named him Chester," she told Emma.

Everyone wanted to tell her how great she did, but Izzy hung back, waiting for the right moment to step in and give her a hug.

"I lost," Emma whispered in her friend's ear.

"You didn't lose. You won second place," Izzy corrected her.

"Then why does it feel so awful?"

Izzy put her hands on her hips. "Okay, what would *Ask Emma* have to say to that?"

Emma sighed. "You can't always win."

"And?" Izzy prodded her.

"And sometimes losing makes you work that much harder to reach your goals."

"And?"

"And we learn much more from our failures than we do from our successes."

"Keep going," Izzy said.

"And lots of brilliant, amazing people have come

in second—like Hillary Clinton. So, you're in good company."

Izzy thought it over. "Yeah, that's a pretty good post. If you check your email, you'll see I asked Emma that exact same question."

Suddenly Emma remembered Izzy had come in second at her gymnastics competition the day before. Of course Izzy understood what Emma was feeling.

"Oh, I'm so sorry, Iz. I forgot," Emma said. "My moping probably made you feel worse."

"No, it actually made me feel better," Izzy admitted. "Because if someone as awesome as my BFF Emma comes in second place, that must be pretty good."

Mr. Hartfield overheard them. "It's better than pretty good. For your first time at the National Student Congress, it's quite an accomplishment. I hope you'll come back next year and participate again."

Emma raised an eyebrow. "Really? You want me to come back? After all the crazy things I did?"

He noticed she was holding a bouquet of roses—

and not sneezing. "Well, faking an allergy to roses was a bit much," he said, winking. "But I won't tell. See you at the gala."

Emma had almost forgotten about the huge banquet, concert, and dance planned for this evening. She had been looking forward to it before, but now it seemed a lot less appealing. "Ugh, I'm sure Aubrey will be there gloating," she told Izzy.

"Well, she doesn't have your dress—expertly styled by your extremely fashionable best friend," Izzy said.

"My power-red dress." Emma smiled.

"With the beaded bodice and chiffon hi-lo skirt," her friend reminded her. "Not to mention the matching red heels. Jackson is going to flip when he sees you."

"If he doesn't hate me for losing the finals," she said. In all the excitement, she hadn't gotten a chance to talk to him or tell him how sorry she was.

Izzy pushed her toward the elevator. "Go get dressed and your fairy godfriends will be up shortly to do your hair and makeup."

Harriet heard her cue. "I brought your fave eye-shadow palate and that frosty gloss you love that tastes like strawberries."

"What would I do without you two?" Emma said, pulling them both in for a hug.

16

A MAGICAL NIGHT

Thanks to Izzy and Harriet, Emma looked like she belonged at a red carpet premiere. They styled her hair in a sophisticated half updo and gave her perfectly smoky eyes and pale pink lips.

"One last little detail," Izzy said, handing her a small velvet box. "A girl should always accessorize." Emma opened it to find a silver pendant, shaped like a crescent moon, studded with a tiny diamond.

Izzy put it around her neck. "Happily ever after to the moon and back," she told Emma. "Now, off to the ball, Cinderella."

When Emma entered the ballroom, she saw that the seats from the Congress were replaced with a light-up dance floor and a shimmering disco ball hung overhead. She spied Jackson in the crowd and their eyes met for a second. Then he looked away and ducked out of sight.

Ugh, he hates me, she thought. *He'll never speak to me again, much less ask me to be his girlfriend.*

Emma saw that Tyler was taking pictures with fans and signing autographs.

"Here ya go—you might want to frame that. It'll be really valuable one day," he was telling a girl from another school. Emma secretly wondered whether anyone had asked Tyler for his signature or if this was his idea.

"I know for a fact he buys his followers on Instagram," someone said in her ear.

Emma spun around to see Aubrey standing behind her. "It's a pretty good bet that he's paying those people to hang all over him tonight."

Emma laughed. "Well, you won. I guess he deserves the attention." She paused to consider why Aubrey would be making fun of her teammate. "But aren't you guys friends?"

Aubrey shrugged. "We're not the kind of friends you and Jackson are."

Emma's eyes widened. Was it *that* obvious that she had a crush on Jax? Could everyone see it? "Well, yeah. We work really well together."

"Congratulations," Aubrey said simply.

"I should be congratulating you. You guys won first place."

"And you put up a really good fight," Aubrey added. "I'm impressed, and I hope we get to debate again next year." She walked away to find her parents and her adviser.

"Did I see you talking to Aubrey?" Jackson asked. He had two glasses in his hands and held one out to her. "I leave you alone for one minute and you're chatting with the enemy?"

She heaved a huge sigh of relief—at least he wasn't avoiding her. He'd gone to get her punch.

"Aubrey's nice," she remarked. "Nicer than you'd guess. She congratulated us."

"Hmm," Jackson replied. "I guess I assumed that everyone who went to Columbus Prep was mean and stuck-up."

Emma glanced over at Tyler, who had now donned a pair of sunglasses to take selfies of himself with the gold medal around his neck. "Yeah well, I can see why you'd think that." She hesitated for a moment. "That and the fact that you were bullied at that school. I get it."

Jackson smiled. "You always get me, Emma."

"I do?" Emma asked. "I mean, I do. I get that you wanted to win, and I'm so sorry we came in second, Jax. It was all my fault."

"No! Second place is amazing for first-timers. We came here to prove ourselves and we more than did that. Besides, there's always next year."

Emma considered his words. "You mean, you'd want to be partners again?"

"Are you kidding? We're the Dream Team!"

Emma noticed how happy and calm Jackson was now that the competition was over. "You seem much more relaxed," she told him.

"I can't believe how nervous I got. I'm lucky you kept a calm, cool head the whole time."

Calm and cool? She wished Ms. Bates could have heard that! She would never have believed it.

"And you look really pretty tonight," he added. "Are you wearing red for Crimson Five?"

Emma laughed. And as if on cue, the band took the stage. The crowd swelled, and Jackson pulled her up to the front with him.

Everyone was cheering, dancing, and singing along. All the competitiveness from the weekend seemed to melt away.

"You never told me your favorite Maroon 5 song," Emma shouted over the music.

Jackson smiled. "This one. It's called 'It Was Always You.'"

Emma's heart did a backflip as she listened to the lyrics: *"It was always you / Can't believe I could not see it all this time . . ."* Was Jackson trying to tell her something? Did he feel this way about her? Or was it a coincidence?

As if he could read her mind, Jackson took her hand and led her to a table in a quiet corner.

"Do you think *Ask Emma* is up for a question?" he asked. "I know it's been a long day. But it's important, and I really could use some help."

Emma nodded—she hoped she knew where this was going. "Of course! How can I help?"

"Well, you see, there's this girl . . . ," Jackson began.

Emma suddenly felt light-headed, like she was floating several feet in the air.

Jackson continued, "I like her but I don't know how to ask her if she wants to go out with me. What should I do?"

"Well," she replied, trying hard to keep her feet

on the ground. "You should tell her how you feel. Be completely honest. Just say, 'Hey, would you maybe like to go out with me sometime?'"

"But what if she doesn't feel the same way?"

"You won't know unless you ask, right?" Emma insisted.

Jackson considered. "Okay, thanks for the advice. I'll keep it in mind." He stood up. "Want to go try that chocolate fountain? It looks yummy."

Emma's heart sank. What? Wasn't he asking *her* out? Wasn't that the point? Or was he interested in some other girl and she'd completely misjudged him?

She started to walk toward the dessert buffet, and he caught her hand in his. "I'm kidding! I've been wanting to ask you forever, so here goes: Hey, would you maybe like to go out with me sometime?"

Emma stared, speechless.

"Yaaas!" cheered a voice from the back of the room. Harriet and Izzy had been spying the entire time—they were hiding behind the chocolate fountain, trying not to be spotted.

"Well, Harriet says yes." Jackson shuffled his feet. "How about you?"

He looked nervous—which made him even more adorable!

"Yes," Emma said, beaming. Jackson smiled back at her. She watched as the disco ball cast tiny lights across the walls and ceiling. It looked like a million shimmering stars.

"Make a wish," he told her.

But her wish had already come true! She'd gotten her perfect day after all—and she didn't need to fix a single thing.

START YOUR OWN
MOTHER-DAUGHTER
BOOK CLUB!

A mother-daughter book club makes reading more fun—and creates a sense of sharing. You gain insight into each other's lives and generations and connect with others in your community. Plus, it's a great way to explore books through creative activities that bring the books' characters and stories to life.

HOW DO I GET STARTED?

To start a club, reach out to your local school, library, religious institution, even a Girl Scout troop, and ask if you can distribute flyers to recruit participants in the area. Once you have a bunch of interested people (five to six mom-daughter pairs, with daughters in the same age range is ideal), decide who will be the first family to host. You can take turns or have one house serve as your club's home base. You can also hold meetings (with permission) in a classroom, library, school lounge, etc. The club organizer should be responsible for circulating the when and where of your meetings (either through email or text message works best) and also encouraging the club to submit ideas for books and activities. Try to include everyone in your club plans—this will make them more excited to be part of each meeting.

HOW OFTEN SHOULD WE MEET?

It's really up to you and depends how busy your members are. A schedule that works for most book clubs is once a month. You will read a book over the course of that month, and plan your activities and discussions around the story you've chosen. The meetings can be anywhere from an hour to two hours long, depending on what you're planning to talk about and do. A cooking activity, for example, will take up a lot of time, so you will need to allot at least an additional 45–60 minutes for your book discussion.

WHAT'S A GOOD THING TO DO AT THE VERY FIRST MEETING?

Easy! Ice breakers! These are games that are aimed at getting everyone to know one another better and stimulating discussions. For example, ask each mom-daughter duo to switch partners with another mom-daughter pair, then have them team up for a game of Never Have I Ever ___, But I Have ___. The key is to make the answers funny and surprising, like "Never have I ever ridden a camel . . . but I have ridden in a hot-air balloon!"

ONCE WE HAVE OUR CLUB . . . THEN WHAT?

Start planning your meetings and choosing your books to read together. On the following pages, you'll find an itinerary we put together if you were reading this book, *Ask Emma: Frenemies*.

MEETING 1

Everyone in the club reads the first half of the book (approximately chapters 1–8) prior to the meeting. The host asks one of the girls in the group to summarize what happened and what she liked most. Get the discussion going by asking questions:

- What are your favorite scenes and why?

- Which character do you relate to the most?

- Emma writes a blog about giving advice because she's so interested in helping others. What would you write a blog about? What kind of blog would you like to read?

- Who are better advice givers, moms or friends?

- Have you ever had a fight with your BFF? What was it about, and how did you solve it?

Now it's activity time!

DIY FRIENDSHIP BRACELETS

A matching set for each mom and daughter—and you can make them for each other.

YOU'LL NEED:

- Several different colors of embroidery floss to choose from. Each bracelet needs approximately 30 inches each of six different colors, so plan accordingly.

- Tape measure

- Scissors

- Safety pins

Measure the circumference of your wrist, then multiply that number by 5. Let's say your wrist is about 6 inches around; you would measure 30 inches of floss in each color. Six colors will make a bracelet that's approximately 1/3″ wide—which is perfect.

Take the 6 strands and tie them all together at one end. Leave about 2 inches of "tail" above the knot. Use a safety pin to secure the strands (place the pin through the knot) to a pillow or even the leg of your jeans. This will keep it firmly in place as you braid and knot. Separate the strands out into the order you want your pattern to be. Grab the first two colors. The strand farthest to the left is going to create your first row. You'll be knotting it around the other strands of floss to achieve this. Let's say your first two strands are orange and red—in that order. Create a number "4" shape with the orange (strand 1) and the red (strand 2) threads. The orange thread will be bent in an L shape over the red thread. The red thread stays straight. Now pull the tail of the orange thread through the center of the "4" to create your first knot. Hold the red thread firmly while you pull on the orange thread.

As you do this, a knot will move up to the top of the red thread. Make a second knot, using the same two threads, the orange one again on top.

Now knot the orange thread (strand 1) twice over each of the other colors until your first row is complete. Remember, a stitch is made of two knots. When you've knotted all of the strands, the orange one will be in the far-right position.

Start the process again with the far-left strand (the red one in our example). Repeat the double-knot technique for each strand to make the next row. Your red strand (and each one after it) will end up on the right when you're done creating the row, and you'll start with a new color of thread every time. Continue until the bracelet is long enough to wrap around your wrist. When it is, tie the second end of the bracelet into a knot. Leave a few inches of "tail" and trim off any excess thread left over.

Now, wrap the bracelet around your mom's (or your daughter's) wrist, and tie the two tails together to secure.

MENU FOR YOUR MEETING

A book club always needs some tasty snacks! Keep yours "themed" to the book; let the plot inspire you. For example, Emma promises Ms. Bates she will be "Switzerland" and stay impartial so she can prove herself a worthy representative at the National Student Congress. Her mom jokes that they should have some Swiss cheese if she's Switzerland—and she grills up a sandwich for the two of them to split.

RECIPE: MINI GRILLED SWISS SAMMYS

INGREDIENTS

- 2 long French baguettes, thinly sliced (one loaf will serve about 4 people)

- 1 lb. Swiss cheese, thinly sliced

- 4–6 tablespoons butter

OPTIONAL INGREDIENTS

- Chopped fresh tomatoes

- Sundried tomatoes

- Apple slices

- Grilled onions

- Turkey or ham slices

- Bacon crumbles

With the help of an adult, use a serrated knife to slice the baguettes crosswise into small, almost round pieces. On one slice, place your cheese and toppings; place a second slice on top and set aside until you're ready to start cooking. Continue until all the bread is used up.

With an adult's help, melt 2–3 tablespoons of butter in a large grill pan. Place your mini sandwiches in the pan, cooking 3–4 minutes on each side until they are toasty and golden brown. You will probably need to grill more than one batch, depending on the size of your slices and your pan.

Serve immediately. Yum!

MEETING 2

The club discusses the second half of the book—focusing on Emma and Jackson's trip to DC and their debating at the Student Congress. Again, ask one club member to sum up the action and start the discussion off with a few questions:

- Which argument do you think was the strongest and which was the weakest? What point would you have made that they didn't?

- Have you ever had a crush on someone? How did it make you feel?

- Jax would like to be president one day. Would you like to be president? Why or why not? And if you were president of the United States, what are some things you would do or change?

- Izzy is disappointed when she comes in second at the state gymnastic competition. How would you feel if you were in her shoes? Have you ever lost at something, and how did it make you feel?

SUGGESTED ACTIVITY: GET ON YOUR FEET!

Emma proves her point about the benefit of physical education in schools by having the audience do jumping jacks. Put on some fun party tunes and have club members participate in this mini-workout challenge. Set up stations (make sure to spread out so you have enough room or take it outside in the backyard) so kids and moms can rotate. Work in teams of moms and daughters, or pit the kids against the grown-ups!

STATION 1: JUMP ROPE

Working in pairs, have one person watch the other for one minute to see how many times she can jump and not miss. Once each person has had a turn, move to the next station.

STATION 2: HULA-HOOP

Set the timer again and challenge each other to keep the hoop on your hips for a minute.

STATION 3: WATER-BOTTLE BICEP CURLS

Take a seat on the edge of a chair or couch, and hold a filled water bottle in each hand (the host provides). Start by holding the bottles down next to the sides of your legs with arms completely straight and palms facing forward. Slowly bend your elbows and curl the bottles up to your shoulders. Hold for a count of three. Now lower the bottles and make sure to straighten your arms all the way until they are next to your legs where you started. Repeat 10 times and rotate so the other person has a turn.

STATION 4: CLIMB THE MOUNTAIN

You can do this one side by side: Start in a push-up position with your arms straight, then alternate bringing one foot at a time forward toward your armpit and then extend it back out. The faster you go, the faster you "climb." Set the timer for a minute and see how many you can do.

STATION 5: FREEZE DANCE

Have a pair operate the music while you and your mom show off your best dance moves until the music stops. Freeze in place and try not to move a muscle. Have your DJ duo judge your performances and pick a dancing queen. Then switch jobs and have them take the dance challenge.

MENU FOR YOUR MEETING: A DIY SMOOTHIE BAR

What could be more fun—and healthy? Lay out all your ingredients and let the club members take turns choosing their faves and blending them. You can use a traditional blender or a smaller version, e.g., a Magic Bullet, to whip up your smoothies (ask club members to bring a small blender if they have them).

SUGGESTED INGREDIENTS:

- Orange juice
- Apple juice
- Plain yogurt
- Vanilla yogurt
- Ripe bananas
- Blueberries
- Strawberries
- Raspberries
- Crushed ice